An Elephant's Journey
Thunder
Hope Haven

Erik Daniel Shein   Melissa Davis

World Castle Publishing, LLC
Pensacola, Florida
Copyright © 2017 Arkwatch Holdings, LLC, and Erik Daniel Shein
Co-Author: Melissa Davis
Hardback ISBN: 9781629898049
Special Edition Hardback ISBN: 9781629896298
Paperback ISBN: 9781629896304
eBook ISBN: 9781629896311
LCN: 2017932567
First Edition World Castle Publishing, LLC, September 5, 2017
http://www.worldcastlepublishing.com
Licensing Notes
Cover: Len Simon Animation, LLC
Illustrator: Paul Barton, II
Editor: Maxine Bringenberg

"If I have ever seen magic, it has been in Africa."
John Hemingway

Dedication

To my late Aunt Bessie Leutenberg. She is always looking down on me.

Table of Contents

CHAPTER 1
NEW BEGINNINGS

As the early morning light filtered through the dense canopy of the Central African rainforest, a chattering chorus of voices came alive. Birds of all kinds were singing their morning salutations, waking the world around them to a new day. The sunlight wove its rays through the canopy of trees above and trickled over the beautiful flowers, bringing out their vivid colors.

The leaves above trembled slightly and a small screech sounded. A flash of fur raced along a branch and was soon followed by another, as two young talapoin monkeys chased each other through the leaves.

A tiny talapoin monkey taunted her brother. "Catch me if you can, loser!"

"Stop! No fair! You run too fast!" He was becoming quite frustrated with his sister. He continued to leap with his tiny legs, but she was still much faster.

"It's not my fault that you're too slow!" She turned around to stick her tongue out at her brother and was almost knocked

7

out of the tree as he collided into her.

"Gotcha!!" Her brother grasped her fur and stuck his tongue out at her.

The pair of them broke into a series of giggles before they reversed roles.

Their mother, in a branch just above them, sighed as she watched them zip across another branch. The mother talapoin turned to her friend in the branch across from her. "At this rate, they'll need a nap by breakfast."

"Hey, don't knock mobility. They could still be stuck to your side." The other female talapoin spoke from experience. At this moment, she had one baby hanging latched onto her furry back.

"Isn't that the truth! Did you hear a screech? Goodness, I wonder what they got into now." The talapoin raced along the branches to find out what calamity had fallen on her children.

"Probably just fell out of the tree again, Lula. I'll come along too." The second talapoin followed her friend with her youngster firmly clutching her back.

Thunder, an African pygmy elephant, watched the two mothers and sighed. Everyone seemed to have happy families, and that element was missing from his life. He had his friends, sure, but it wasn't the same. Thunder yearned for a mate to complete his life, yet he seemed, instead, to journey from one adventure to the next.

When he was still a young calf, Thunder had been separated from his herd by poachers and had traveled across Central Africa to find his way home. While it had not started off as a grand adventure, Thunder had found himself traveling with four feathered friends and a cantankerous rhino. They had helped him reunite with his herd and his mother.

Then when he was a little older, another quest came out of the most tragic of circumstances. When his mother became a casualty to a frenzied stampede, Thunder found himself at an unfortunate crossroads. As he had mourned her loss, his despair was so great that he had left everything and everyone he had ever known behind. Thankfully, his friends had not given up on him, and he had been fortunate to make even more friends along the way.

He might have left the herd a little younger than other elephants, but he was not alone. His friends were always happy to keep him company. Today, Thunder was checking to see if any of the birds wanted to go for a small adventure to the beach. It had been some time since they had been there and Thunder was hankering for adventure, as he often did.

Thunder took a few steps and walked closer to Sydney's nest. He heard a few voices, none that sounded anything like Sydney.

"Hey! Ouch! Idi!!" came Lumo's tiny voice.

"Watch it, will ya?" Awiti complained.

"I can't help it if I need more room." Idi shuffled against his siblings.

"Knock it off!" Lumo attempted to move away from his brother. His quick movements caused Idi to bump into his sister.

Awiti tumbled over the side of the nest, screaming, "AAAHHHHH!!!"

She had not learned how to fly yet. Her wings moved in

frenzied flaps. Thunder reached out and caught her with his trunk before she hit the ground. Awiti snuggled close against him, her heart racing. "Thunder! Oh my gosh, thank you!"

"No problem, Awiti." Thunder lifted her up and gently placed her in the nest. "Idi! What would your mama say?"

"B-b-but Uncle Thunder, I didn't mean to." His beak seemed to tremble at the thought of his mother's reactions when she found out.

"That may be, but you could have really hurt your sister." Thunder put his trunk up and ruffled Idi's feathers. The tiny egrets were enough to melt his heart. Their bodies were still more fluff than feathers. Thunder imagined that they would look a lot like Sydney when their feathers came in. Sydney was one of three egrets who had befriended Thunder when he was much younger. This was Sydney's third brood, and while she loved motherhood, she let her mate do the majority of the work.

"Where is your mama?" Thunder asked them.

Awiti scratched her neck with her foot. "She went out."

"For food?" Thunder should not have mentioned that word, for as soon as he did, Lumo started to hop up and down excitedly.

"Fooooooooooddd!" Lumo's mouth opened and closed as if he were imagining the tasty bugs Sydney would bring back.

Awiti sniffed in irritation. "Is that all you think about?"

"Well…yes!" Lumo stuck his beak up at her.

Thunder chuckled. These three birds were so much like the other egrets Sydney, Persius, and Cedric. Sydney and

10

Persius had several offspring, but Cedric had never been able to find a mate. Thunder could certainly relate. Finding the right mate was hard. The fates had to align perfectly to make the right match. Cedric had become the goofy uncle to his siblings' kids. He seemed to like that, as did Thunder, for while he was not an egret he was an honorary member of their family.

Thunder enjoyed spending time with the youngsters, but today he was on a mission. "Well, if you see your mama, let her know I am heading to the beach. She knows where to find me."

"Okay, Uncle Thunder." Idi moved closer to the edge of the nest so that he could run his beak along Thunder's trunk.

Thunder smiled and lifted his trunk back up. Before he knew it, all three of them were hugging him tight in adoration. His heart felt light, filled to the brink with their innocent love. "Okay. Bye now."

The three hatchlings moved back away from him and settled back into their nest. Thunder made sure they were safe before he moved away. He moved through the next line of trees and shook the branch above him. A large nest was perched on top.

A loud squawk sounded. "What?!"

Thunder snorted slightly. "Wake up, Cedric."

The egret peered over his nest and rolled his eyes. "Did you have to wake me up? I was having the best dream ever. Something about flamingos in tutus, and some lovely egrets doing the hula in leafy skirts."

"O—kay…," Thunder chuckled at his friend. "That does

11

sound like quite a dream. Sounds like something Frederick would come up with."

"No doubt. Why are you waking me up at the crack of dawn?" Cedric's white plumage was quite tousled from his sleep. He slid his wing over it to smooth it down slightly.

"I thought we should take a trip." Thunder was not sure Cedric would want to go. From here it looked like he had woken up on the wrong side of the nest.

Cedric started to preen his feathers with his beak. He smoothed down a few and spoke through his feathers. "Oh? Where to? Does it involve any bachelorettes?"

Thunder rolled his eyes. Sometimes Cedric had a one-track mind. While Thunder wanted a mate to share his life with too, he did not think about it every second of the day. "Highly unlikely, unless egrets have started to hang out at the beach."

"Hmmm…." Cedric looked around him as if he were checking out his prospects. "Well, there aren't any here either. Can I catch a ride?"

"Sure. I tried to get Sydney, but she was away from her nest. Do you know if Persius is around?"

"Nah. He flew to the opposite end of the rainforest. He's on egg duty right now. Last I heard, they could hatch at any moment." Cedric flew down from his nest and landed on top of Thunder's back.

"Well, the others said they would meet us at the trail. Ready to go?" Thunder turned his head as he addressed Cedric.

"Lead on, fearless leader." Cedric moved closer to

Thunder's head, turned around, and lay his head down. He crossed his long spindly legs out in front of him and put his wings under his head. "Ah…this is the life."

CHAPTER 2
MEASURING UP

By the time Thunder reached the trail where they were going to meet the others, it was nearing lunch time. His stomach was rumbling loudly. A loud gurgle shook his midsection, waking the egret on his back. "Sorry, Cedric. I guess I'm hungrier than I thought."

"I'll say. Maybe we should stop for a bite," suggested Cedric. He was looking at the trees around them.

Thunder noticed Cedric appeared to be looking for more than food and smirked. "Right…on the prowl again, Cedric?"

Cedric's beak spread into a huge grin. "Well…I thought I saw a few white feathers over that way." He shrugged innocently. "I think it might be worth a look."

"Fine," Thunder chuckled. "Whatever. The others should be here soon anyway, so don't go too far. I think I'll scrounge up something while we're waiting." Thunder watched as Cedric flew into the trees. He turned to the nearest tree and started to pick the bark off it. He used his left tusk to scrape as much off as he could. The tree shook slightly as he rubbed up against it.

"Hey! Do you mind?"

Startled, Thunder looked up to see a white-throated blue swallow sticking his head over its nest with his wing raised threateningly. His blue head glistening where the sun hit it.

"Sorry!" Thunder moved away from the tree apologetically.

"You do know that we need these trees too, right? Take too much bark and you might as well put a rest in peace sign on the tree," he grumbled at Thunder.

"I never take more than I need," Thunder tried to explain, but it was clear that the bird simply wanted to complain. Thunder stepped back and raised his trunk up in salutation. "Have a nice day, sir."

More muffled complaints came, but at this point Thunder had tuned them out. He was still hungry and decided to dig for tubers instead. By the time he had eaten his fair share, his friends had started to arrive.

Razor padded up next to him. The lion shook out his mane before he greeted him. "Afternoon."

Thunder grinned. "About time!" He moved his trunk over to Razor's ears and blew out a hot breath of air. His mane flew in several different directions. Thunder considered trumpeting, but did not want to hurt Razor's ears.

Razor tackled his trunk and tried to roll Thunder to the ground, but he was quite outsized. The lion ended up falling to the ground with a thud. Razor rubbed his hip with his paw. "Ouch."

16

"Well that was close." A tiny head popped out of Razor's mane. Archie crossed his arms over his chest. "A little warning next time?"

Thunder lowered his trunk to the black banded lizard. "Sorry. Archie. I didn't realize you were there."

"I'm incognito. I think I saw Rita hanging in the trees back there. That's one crazy dame. I swear, you go on one date and suddenly she's talking children." Archie made a disgusted look.

"Good. We already have enough Archie juniors running around this jungle," teased Razor.

A genet darted through the nearest bush. His cat-like body was covered in soft gray fur that was dotted with black spots along the spine. Two little furballs rolled through the brush and landed in a clumsy heap at Thunder's feet. "Sorry I took so long. The missus requested I bring the children this time. Something about needing some me time."

"No problem, Dash."

Thunder scooped up one of the kits with his trunk and inspected her. The young genet attempted to box his trunk with her paws. Thunder tossed her up into the air and her legs sprawled out around her as she tried to prepare herself for landing.

"Hey, watch it! Will ya!"

Thunder caught her and tossed her up in the air again. This time her little brother pounced on his foot. "Let her go!"

Thunder giggled as the kit's teeth tickled his skin. He put the other kit down safely next to him. "They're still quite young, aren't they? Will they be able to make the journey with us okay?"

"We are not! Tell him, Papa."

"Hush, Khari. No one doubts your courage, lad." Dash ruffled his son's fur.

"Papa, I'm brave too. Did you see! I flew through the air." Ayo puffed out her chest.

"Yes, dear girl. I saw," Dash chuckled. Before Dash could say more, Khari tackled Ayo and the two went tumbling through the air. They rolled all over the place before they smashed into the tree nearby.

"How do you sleep?" asked Archie. The lizard appeared a little leery of the children.

"Like the dead...." Dash snickered. "The missus usually wakes up with them."

"No wonder she needs me time."

At this point the two genets were rolling a small ball of something around the ground, passing it back and forth.

Thunder sniffed the air. "What is that smell?"

"Please tell me they aren't playing with poop again." Dash hung his head in frustration.

"Poop! Please tell me you're joking!" Archie put a finger over his nose and held his nostrils shut.

At this point, Thunder could not help the laughter that was building inside him. The very thought of anyone playing with their poop had turned Archie nearly a shade of green. "That's hilarious."

Razor joined in. He was laughing so hard he collapsed on the ground. His large paws beat on the ground in emphasis. "You should see your face! Ah-ha-ha-ha! Cedric, you can come down now."

Cedric flew down from the tree above him. He whistled slightly as he landed. "Morning."

"Man, Cedric! What did you eat?" Razor put a paw to his face and waved the smelly fumes away from his face.

"Oh, I didn't break wind. This is my new cologne." Cedric sat up on Thunder's back with a proud look on his face.

"What did you do, squeeze stink bugs all over yourself?" Archie looked like he was about to barf.

"Well, I figured it couldn't hurt." Cedric shrugged his shoulders.

"Well, it sure can't help either." Dash shook his head.

"How many attempts does this make?" Archie asked curiously.

"I dunno. I gave up after the first hundred." Dash wrinkled his nose.

"It's only been thirty-seven. Give me some credit, will ya?" Cedric shook his head at his friends.

"You'll find someone, Cedric." Thunder wanted to tell them to stop talking, but he did not have the heart to do so. Cedric was not the only animal here who did not have a mate, after all. They may not realize how difficult it was for their friends to find mates of their own. This was a sore subject for both of them.

Razor looked at Thunder perceptively. He rolled his eyes at the other two and quickly changed the topic. "So, who's surfing today?"

"Not me...," Cedric gestured to himself. "It would be a waste of cologne to get in the water."

Razor got closer to Thunder and whispered to him, "Please tell me you can spray him down."

Thunder chuckled softly and whispered back, "I can if I can catch him by surprise. He hides every time I get close to water."

Razor chuckled with him, remembering the last time Thunder sprayed Cedric down. Cedric's feathers were sticking up in every direction. The more he thought about it, the harder he laughed.

Thunder held his breath as he patted Cedric on the head with his trunk. "Stranger things have been known to happen, Cedric." Thunder tried to encourage Cedric.

"Right...." Cedric smiled and tapped Thunder's back. "I met this amazing egret just now. She would have been mine, but some Don Juan stepped in at the last moment."

"Sorry, pal. Next time?" Dash gave Cedric a half-smile.

Cedric shrugged. "One day I'll have to get it right. For now though, off to another grand adventure!" Cedric put a wing up into the charge position.

"If you call a day sitting at the beach an adventure," Archie snickered.

"Papa, did he say beach?" Ayo jumped up and down. "I've always wanted to see the beach."

"Right. Thunder, do you mind?" Dash gestured to his offspring.

"Of course not." Thunder lowered his trunk and gathered the two genets, then tossed them up into the air.

"Wheeeee!" the two of them cried, and both looked disappointed when they landed with a dull thud on Thunder's back.

"Off to the beach," Thunder declared.

"Hey, it beats weaving more sticks into one of my nests. I'm up to six now. Maybe I need to mix some bling into them like Frederick suggested. But, alas…that is neither here nor there."

Thunder let out a soft sigh. The more they talked about Cedric's woes, the more it made Thunder want to stomp his feet on the ground. He decided to keep quiet though. Thankfully, as soon as they started moving, the banter stopped. The trees opened wider and the trail to the beach was now exposed. The sandy shores were the closest thing to snow any of them had ever seen. The white granules sparkled in the sun's rays.

Thunder turned around to find Dash wrapping small leaves around his paws. "What are you doing?"

Dash gestured to his legs. "Protecting my paws. One of the gorillas told me the uprights sometimes wear things on their feet to protect their skin. I thought it might work for my paws."

"I never have a problem," Razor declared.

"Well, you have more fur on your feet than I do." Dash took a few tentative steps on the sand. When the leaves held onto his feet, he seemed content. "Ahhh!! So much better. Children, come down so I can wrap your paws too.

Ayo and Khari slid down Thunder's trunk and landed in a heap at their father's feet. He quickly fashioned small shoes for them. The two of them followed right behind him. Their eyes were wide with wonder.

As they walked down the beach, as always, Thunder was

21

reminded of his mother, Serenity. The last adventure they had together had been right here at this beach. One of the hippos had asked to measure their feet. To this day, the large circle remained in the garden of feet the hippo kept farther up the banks.

"You guys go ahead. I'll be right there." Thunder left the group and headed to the garden of feet that had grown over the years. Shapes made with rocks, shells, sticks and other debris lined the garden from top to bottom. In a way, this was like a grave marker for Serenity. It was far easier to remember her during her life than the tragic way she had died.

Thunder pulled a flower from the edge of the rainforest and brought it back to the foot garden. He placed it on Serenity's print and let out a soft sigh. "I miss you, Mother. I think I always will."

There was so much he felt he had missed out on when she passed away. The gentle nudging into young adulthood might have prepared him a little better for the loneliness he might feel when he was estranged from his herd. When male elephants reached a certain age, they had to head out to find their own lives, while the females were able to stay within their herds. Some of the male elephants would run around in small bachelor herds and some would stay alone. Thunder fell into the second category, except for the fact he had enough friends to keep loneliness at bay.

Thunder lifted his foot and let it hover over Serenity's. His had now surpassed hers by a few inches. He had always thought following in her footsteps would be a difficult task. While she was physically gone, he did often feel her presence near him. Thunder had actually heard her voice when he visited the caves, but that had only happened once. Her last words were for him to find Hope Haven and his destiny.

Hope Haven was still a mystery to Thunder. He had searched for it, but had no idea what to look for. None of the animals knew what Hope Haven was. Thunder had tried returning to the caves to see if he would get any clues from his mother's spirit, but she had not come back to him.

Thunder let his trunk touch the sand inside the footprint. "Someday I will find Hope Haven, Mother. I won't give up until I do."

As Thunder walked down the beach, he heard a commotion from the ocean. An unusual cry echoed across the winds. He turned to see a large orca whale in the distance. A thick gush of water spouted from it and shot high into the air. Thunder had never seen a whale before. The orca whale dove under the water. In moments, his body jumped through the air and he landed on his back. Thunder watched the water shake around him. For some reason, the sight of such a magnificent creature lifted his spirits. Perhaps, it was a sign that he was finally going to head in the right direction.

CHAPTER 3
SURF'S UP!

As Thunder walked across the beach, he could see that the hippos were up to something again. His friends were watching from a few feet away. Thunder moved closer to them. "What are they doing?"

"I don't know exactly. I think I heard one of them say mancala." Razor gestured to the hippo on the end.

"What is mancala?" Thunder had never heard that word before.

"It's a game the uprights play," Dash answered.

"What's an upright?" Ayo asked her father curiously.

"Uhm…well…an upright is like an animal who walks on two feet," Dash tried to explain.

"Like Cedric? Are you an upright?" Khari tilted his head as he stared closely at the egret.

"Me? Good heavens, no." Cedric blustered before them.

"Uprights do not have wings, or much fur for that matter. They build their nests above the ground." At this point, the children had lost interest.

"All right, so back to this mala fala thing." Archie pointed to the hippos.

"Man-cala, Archie," Dash chuckled slightly.

"How in the world do you know that?" Archie slid down Razor's back, climbed down his tail, and landed on the small boulder next to him.

"Well, the missus listens to all the gossip. Apparently, some of the gorillas know how to play. Maybe they taught the hippos," suggested Dash.

"That's always possible. I bet it was Harold and Neville. They always seem to know how humans do things. Maybe they feel a kinship with them, being able to walk on two feet sometimes." Thunder's ears flapped gently against his sides and his tail flicked away a few sand fleas.

Thunder watched the two hippos standing near a long log. On the log were twelve large shells placed by twos. There were two long oval indentations on the top and bottom of the log. The shells were filled with tiny pebbles that tiny bonobos chimps were moving around for the hippos.

"All right there, move my marbles, will ya, Taz?" Rudy gestured to the marbles in the closest shell. When the bonobos had moved each of his marbles, the hippo smiled. "Thanks, Taz. I think we'll win yet!"

Jemma, the hippo standing at the opposite side of the board, was clearly not ready to concede. "Bah. So you say, old timer! Max, give them a toss."

The tiny bonobos turned to the hippo and saluted. "Aye! Aye!"

Another group of hippos was standing nearby, and they

seemed a little disgruntled. "Do you mind? You're hogging the board!"

"Well, it wouldn't be a problem if we had another one," the oldest hippo answered.

Inspiration struck Thunder instantly. He called to the hippos from where he stood. "I have an idea. If I can find another log, we could make another board together."

"Thunder!" Dale was an adolescent hippo that Thunder had seen here a few times. He was happy to see Thunder. He raced over to where Thunder stood.

"Hello, Dale." Thunder smiled warmly at him.

"Hi! And hello to all of you. Did you mean what you just said?" Dale's eyes were wide with excitement.

"Yeah. All I have to do is find a falling tree or some large debris. There's always plenty on the beach around here." Thunder pointed up and down the stretch of beach with his trunk.

"Great!" Dale was clearly excited.

"Razor, you come with me. Dash and Archie, you are on shell duty. Maybe you can convince Cedric to go find some small rocks for us." Thunder nodded to where the bird was lounging in a tree.

"Sounds like a plan," agreed Dash. "Come along, children."

Thunder and Razor made their way up and down the shore line. They were not having much luck finding a piece of bark, so Thunder decided to go a little further into the trees. Razor had stayed on the beach to keep checking. Before long, Thunder found a dead tree that was close to falling completely over. He pushed against it a few times and stepped back as it crashed.

He used his tusk to sever the last few splinters that kept it attached to the stump. Then he wrapped his trunk around the base and carried it carefully through the trees. The log was easy for him to manage; even though it was pretty wide, the insides were hollow.

Thunder made his way to where Dale was standing. "Okay. Now, all we gotta do is split it. Stand back!" The others moved back as he dropped the log on the ground. He raised his front legs and stomped on the log as hard as he could. The log splintered and cracked before splitting right open. "There!"

"Good job, Thunder!" Dale was visibly excited. "Okay, let's put the shells down here. Looks like we have enough for two extra boards. That's so awesome!"

Thankfully, the animals had gathered more than enough materials to make the boards. They used some of the tree sap inside the log to attach the shells. Instead of long grooves inside the log, they improvised and used a few shells to create the longer indentation. Once this was accomplished, the new mancala games were good to go.

Thunder watched them for a bit, but did not really want to play. Dash and Archie were having a blast using the extra board. The young genets were chucking marbles into the trees, trying to knock Cedric from his perch. As Thunder started to walk away he heard a loud squawk. He turned to find a very red-faced egret fuming from the tree tops.

"Ouch!" Cedric turned around and shook his wingtip at

them. "Knock it off!"

"We were trying to, but we missed you," Khari called up at him.

Cedric tore a branch from the tree and waved it in the air. "If you know what's good for you—"

"What? You'll build us a nest?" Ayo giggled uncontrollably.

Cedric rolled his eyes and dropped the stick. "I think I'll try my luck further up the beach."

Then he heard the squabbling voices of Dash and Archie as they fought over their rocks. Razor seemed to have it under control though.

"Hey, hey. No cheating!" Razor was keeping the pair of them in line. He pulled Archie up by the tail and set him away from Dash. Archie was trying to lunge at the genet. Razor shook his head. "And I thought I'd have to babysit the children."

From across the shore, Thunder saw the faint outline of a large shape followed by a smaller one. He was pretty sure he knew who the larger shape was. "Riley!"

"Hello, little man. How are the waves, Thunder?" the hippo called to him.

Thunder left his friends to their game and made his way over to Riley. The shape following behind him was actually a young hippo. "I haven't been in the water yet. Who is this little guy?"

"This is my progeny, Hai. Hai, this is Thunder." Riley nodded from his son to Thunder.

"Thunder? *The* Thunder? Oh my goodness, I can't wait to tell my friends. They are so not going to believe this. I get to

surf with Thunder. Oh, they are going to be sooooo jealous."
Hai was very excited. His tiny ears twisted a few times and
his mouth opened to show a toothy smile that spread from
one end of his face to another.

"Nice to meet you too, Hai." Thunder put his trunk on
Hai's head and ruffled his skin lightly. "You're very lucky to
have a father like Riley."

"Oh, I knos! He's the best!" Hai agreed.

"That's awfully kind of you, Thunder." Riley walked to
where the tide was ripping across the sand. "Now, the first
part is tricky, Hai. You have to get used to the rhythm of the
waves."

Hai followed his father into the frothy white water. He
giggled as the waves ran across his legs. "That tickles!"

Thunder had to agree. The water did tickle when it first
hit the legs. "Yes. It does."

"All right, Thunder. Can you stay in front of Hai, and I'll
go behind him?" Riley asked him.

"Sure."

The pair of them guided the young hippo safely into the
ocean. When they got a little farther out in the water, Hai's
face became filled with fear.

"What is that!!" He nodded to the small shape that was
coming closer to them.

The closer it got, the larger the shape became. For a
moment, Thunder thought it might be a shark or manatee,
but then it burst from the water and arced over their heads.
Thunder watched in awe. "What is that?"

"A dolphin." Riley had a relaxed smile on his face. "That's

my buddy, Chance."

"A dolphin?" Thunder had never seen one before. He had only heard about them from the other animals on the beach. He watched as Chance swam around and stuck his head out of the water.

A light giggly laugh rang out as Chance shook his head back and forth. "Greetings, water dudes."

"How's it hanging, Chance?" Riley lifted up a foot and held it out for Chance to bump his nose against.

"Awesome, totally. Perfect waves today." Chance moved to his back and glided backwards in the water.

"Right on, bruh. I'm teaching Hai to surf today."

"No way! This is Hai?" Chance ducked under the water and swam closer. When he was right in front of Hai, he rose up and squirted him with water.

Hai caught on right away and slammed his face in the water, splashing the dolphin. The two of them had a mini splash war until Riley interrupted them. "Time to catch a wave!"

Thunder went to Hai's side and helped the other two guide him through the waters. The four of them rode the wave to the beach, with Hai giggling all the way. They continued to surf for a good part of the afternoon. When they were finished, they dried off on the beach. Hai went to join the other hippos that were sunning themselves on the sand, leaving Thunder and Riley alone.

"So, how are things, Thunder?" Riley asked him.

"Well, good I suppose." Thunder's heart was heavy. He had never told Riley about Serenity's words to him in the cave. He wondered if he should.

"Come on, bruh. If you suppose, that means you're not sure. Happiness is not something you question. It's something you know. You have to feel it. What do *you* feel?"

"Well, lost, lonely I suppose. You see, I was told a while ago that I should be pursuing my destiny." Thunder sighed.

"You've always been on the road to your destiny, Thunder. The Great Tusker has been watching you from the moment you were born." Riley nodded to the sky above.

There was a Great Tusker in the sky that all the animals believed in. It was a higher power that looked out for the animals in their world. Thunder also believed in his powers. "But if the Great Tusker wants me to find Hope Haven, why hasn't he shown me where it is?"

"Hope Haven?" Riley's voice was curious.

"Yes. I was told that my next journey would be Hope Haven, but I have no clue what it is. Have you ever heard of it?" Thunder was hopeful that Riley might have the answers.

"No, I have not, but I do know of a place where you might find some answers. There's an animal named Spiro, who lives in Crystal Lagoon. From what I hear, he's quite the traveler. He may know where Hope Haven is and what you might find there."

"Oh? Where is Crystal Lagoon?" Thunder had never heard of it before.

"Head southeast through the rainforest. When you find the tree that's wider than yourself, you will find the entrance to the Crystal Lagoon," Riley answered him.

For the first time in years, Thunder felt relieved. He wished he would have asked Riley a long time ago, but Thunder knew that things happened in their own time. Perhaps now was the time to finally find out what the Great Tusker had in store for him.

"Thank you, Riley." Thunder smiled at his friend.

"Any time, little man," Riley answered him. To the hippo, Thunder would always be that young calf that he had met all those years ago.

CHAPTER 4
DEVIOUS CLAN

In the darkest recess of the rainforest, trouble was just waking up. A pair of glowing eyes could be seen inside the small cave. Delphi sniffed the air and sat up. Sensing her movement, her clan started to rise too. Her offspring Tara, Simone, and Jack were still with her, as none had offspring of their own yet.

"What?" Jack asked her.

Tara smacked him in the head with her paw. "Manners?"

"Ouch! You don't have to hit so hard!" Jack put his head down on the ground and rubbed it with his paws. He gave his sister the evil eye.

"Yes...I do. Otherwise, you repeat the question." Tara raised a paw and threatened to hit him again.

As she started to walk by him, he swung his leg under hers and she fell on her behind. "Walk much?" he taunted her.

"Children...." Delphi silenced them with one word.

Simone sat up and shook her head at her siblings.

35

"Amateurs."

"That is why you're my first born," agreed Delphi. She was proud of her daughter Simone. One day she would make a fine leader. Simone was calm and collected when it called for it, but the minute anyone thought to cross her, Simone was capable of putting any foe in their place.

Simone bowed her head in respect, while giving her two siblings a nasty smile. "Live to serve, Mother."

"It's time to put our plan into action. Now that we have an undeniable force, we will bring justice to our kind and get that elephant once and for all," Delphi decreed. Today, they would gather all the clans together. Then she would finally have her one true wish, to bring down a pachyderm who had been like a thorn in her side for years.

"Oh goodie!" Jack sat up and rubbed his paws together. "I get the left leg."

"Which one? He has two of them." Tara was also imagining her feast.

"I'll take the front, you take the back?" suggested Jack.

"Deal," Tara agreed.

Simone rolled her eyes in the darkness. "You'll get what Mother decides. We'll also be sharing with the others. Don't get greedy."

"And that is why she'll be the next leader. You two have little promise." Delphi was filled with disgust. How had she gone so wrong in their upbringing? Had she been too soft on them?

Jack and Tara scrunched their noses at Simone and grumbled softly. Simone ignored them and turned to face the entrance to the cave. "Shall I gather the others?"

"Yes. We'll meet at Skull Pillar." Delphi stood up and stretched her back in a long arch. When she'd worked all the kinks out of her bones she started to move to the entrance, but stopped mid tracks. "Did you hear that?"

"Huh?" Jack was oblivious.

"Quiet, fool!"

Delphi turned her head and listened. She heard a slight whispering sound that sounded like movement, but it was coming from behind the cave walls, or maybe even under her feet. There were tiny cracks here and there in the rocks all around them, but nothing to be concerned with really. None of them had slid inside any of them before.

Delphi put her head down to the nearest crack and closed one eye so that she could see closely out of the other. Running her head along the crack, she looked for any sign of movement. She thought she saw something orange go by, but could not be certain. She stood up and blinked a few times to adjust her eyes again.

After a few seconds, Delphi decided she must have imagined it, for the sound no longer could be heard. "Must be the wind."

"Well, it's not the bats. They flew the coop when we came in." Tara nodded to the ceiling and chuckled. She pretended to be a bat and hopped around on her hind legs, while her front legs waved around her.

"Yeah, one look at your ugly face and they were scarred for life," Jack snickered.

Tara growled low before leaping through the air. The two

of them rolled around on the ground snapping at each other's throats.

Delphi turned and snarled at them. The two of them stood up and assumed a respectful position.

"Fools...never underestimate any foe."

"Yes, Mother." They both answered and saluted her.

Delphi let out an irritated sigh. "We move." When they did not immediately move, Delphi snapped at them. "NOW!"

The two hyenas yelped at her words and sprang into action. They tripped over each other as they tried to take up their spots behind her, staying on her flank as Delphi started to move from the cave. Each one kept their eyes trained on the sides of Delphi, to seek out any potential threat to her.

A small blue duiker was grazing nearby. Upon seeing the hyenas proceeding through the forest, the tiny antelope shivered in her spot. When she finally got past her nerves, she darted into the overgrowth to hide from view. The hyenas could easily have taken the duiker down, but they were on a mission. Whenever Delphi gave an order, it was wise to follow it with no distractions.

Before long, they made it to their destination. Skull Pillar was a large boulder that resembled the shape of a hyena skull. Over time, the sides of the boulder had been naturally sculpted by the elements, leaving small indentations where eye sockets might appear. The hyenas had used the rock to sharpen their claws over time, leaving imprints along the shape of the jawline that made tiny imprints resembling teeth.

Delphi leapt onto Skull Pillar and looked down at her hyena clan that had grown to massive proportions. That had taken a lot of work on her part. Whenever a leader could overturn others, they earned the right to stand on Skull Pillar and reign over the clans in the region. "Friends, I have earned the right to be your leader. I have fought your fiercest, battled any foe you put before me. Now, it is time for us to come together for a united cause. I stand on Skull Pillar as a reminder that what we want is worth fighting for. The plains are filled with bountiful food, but one animal eludes us. Thunder...." Small yelps and nervous laughter broke out around her. "Yes, I know he does not travel alone, but there are more of us than there are of them. Who is with me?"

At first there was a collective silence. Delphi's offspring were in the crowd though. Wherever they saw dissent, they would gnash their teeth, snarl at their quarry, or even give a nasty swipe of their claws. Before long, the hyenas were answering her. None of them really wanted to take on the legendary Thunder.

One hyena whispered to his friend. "But it's Thunder... they say he makes the ground quake like a powerful god."

"Yes, I've seen it. He can pull lightning from the sky and smite us at will." His friend trembled next to him.

Simone swiped her paw at the first hyena. "Shut up, you fool! That is not true! There is nothing special about him. Nothing at all."

The hyena looked at her in disbelief. "Right...."

Simone snarled at him and her fur rose all the way down her spine. "Do you dare argue with me?"

The hyena yelped in fear as Delphi sprung just behind her daughter. "No, no, Simone. Of course not."

39

"I didn't think so." Simone turned to face her mother and gave her a knowing smile.

Delphi returned the gesture, and nodded for Simone to follow her. The pair moved away from the clan. "I've seen Thunder's group. Our clan has been watching them quite closely these days. If they do not change course, we'll be able to catch up with them quickly enough near Crocodile Rocks. If we corner them at the water's edge, they will have no choice. They'll either be our food, or sink to the bottom of the river."

"Let's hope they stay on land then." Simone's tongue licked the outside of the lips as she imagined the tasty meat she would be feasting on.

The pair of them moved across the crowd of hyenas and Delphi jumped back on the rock. She started to give out orders for each smaller clan of hyenas. "You'll come from the east. Dodger, from the west. We'll come together when they least expect it. Now, let's run."

CHAPTER 5
TRAVELING COMPANIONS

The air was filled with the smell of fresh blooming flowers as the small group returned back from the beach. Thunder had always loved their soft petals. He picked one from a nearby plant and held it up to look at it as he continued to walk.

A tree frog hopped across their path and turned to them. "Excuse me! Coming through."

"Pardon me," Thunder excused himself. If the frog had not warned him, Thunder might have stepped on him.

Ayo and Khari sprang into action. The two genets raced after the frog, disappearing into the brush. Thunder leaned over and watched to see what they were up to. The pair of them were watching the frog intently.

"Stay still, Ayo." Khari put a paw up to warn her. He was watching the frog intently.

The frog turned around and faced them. He looked like he was trying not to let his nerves get the best of him. The genets were predators, after all. "What are you doing?"

"Watching you hop," Ayo answered cheerfully.

"O…kay. Why?" The frog looked at her as if she had lost her mind.

"So we can hop too, duh!" Ayo shook her head at the frog.

"Right…." The frog looked up at Thunder and gave him a half-grimaced smile.

Thunder shrugged his shoulders. "You got me."

"Well then. If you'll excuse me, I'll just be going now." The frog hopped away as fast as his little body would carry him.

"I bet I can hop higher than you, Ayo." Khari sat back on his hind legs, then sprang forward with his front legs. His body, unused to the odd movement, went crashing to the ground head first. When he looked up, he had dirt on his nose.

Ayo burst into high-pitched squeals. "That was hilarious!"

"I'd like to see you do better," Khari grumbled.

"Ha! You're on." Ayo perched like the frog, and when her body leapt into the air, she nearly jumped over Karhi's head. Her legs caught on her brother and soon both of them were rolling all over the ground.

Thunder shook his head and smiled. He turned away from the two of them and wondered how long it would take before one of them poked an eye out. He was relieved when Dash came over to handle the situation. As they continued to walk, his mind wandered. There was so much he needed to do, and watching the little genets reminded him that there was no time to waste.

Razor looked over at him. "You seem distracted today, Thunder."

"I suppose I am." Thunder searched for the words to

43

describe the melancholy he often hid inside. While he shared many things with his friends, his mother's words had not been something he felt comfortable disclosing. Thunder stopped and faced Razor. "When we were at the beach, I told Riley about Hope Haven."

"Hope Haven? What is that?" Dash asked him. His small face was turned up to him in curiosity.

"I'm not sure. But I think it must be a special place. I've been looking for it for a while now," Thunder sighed.

"Really? And why is this the first time we have heard of it?" Cedric tapped a foot on Thunder's back.

"Well, I wasn't sure what to say. How does one tell his friends his dead mother told him to find a place no one has ever heard of?"

Cedric flew off his back and grabbed his trunk. The egret hugged it close to him as he tried to keep in the air. "Serenity spoke to you?"

"Yes. A while ago, actually." Thunder grabbed Cedric to steady him and set him back on his head.

"Why didn't you tell me, Thunder?" Razor looked concerned. Sometimes the lion still felt responsible for her death. While Thunder had forgiven him for causing the stampede, there would always be a part of him waiting for Thunder to hate him again.

"Because I thought it would make you feel bad." Thunder gave Razor a half smile. "And you shouldn't, because that is all in the past. Besides…how crazy does it sound that I would be talking to the dead?"

"It's not so different than carrying on a conversation with

an African gray parrot. At least you'd get a full sentence from your mom," teased Archie. "How is Penelope these days?"

"A little frazzled, from what I could tell last time I saw her. The poor parrot is being run over by her brood real fast. Nothing better than watching four hatchlings mimicking a bird that spends half her time saying the craziest things. She seemed quite unhinged when I went to visit," Cedric chuckled.

"Awe! I didn't know the eggs had hatched. Why didn't you say so? The missus would have loved to see the tiny ones. She's just got baby fever all the time.... Although, maybe she should stay away. I'm not in a rush to add more to our family. These two keep me busy enough." Dash's two kits were racing through the trees. Apparently their need for speed matched his.

"I hear ya!" Archie's face was also filled with mild panic at the thought of more offspring.

Thunder laughed at the pair of them. They may act like they would rather revert back to their bachelor lifestyles, but Thunder knew better. "Right. So, none of you have heard of Hope Haven?"

"Nope," Cedric answered.

"What about the Crystal Lagoon?" Thunder asked them. At first none of them responded, but then Archie did.

"Well, I think I've heard it whispered through the leaves sometimes. It's a place where the water is crystal clear. You can see all the way down to the very bottom. It's so secluded from the outside world that the silence inside is almost deafening. Why?"

"Well, when we were at the beach, Riley told me that I might find an animal named Spiro who lives there. He might know where to find Hope Haven." Thunder snagged a few berries from the tree next to him as he walked. He brought the them to his mouth and peeled them off the twig before tossing it to the ground.

At this point, they were just reaching Cedric's nest. He hopped from Thunder's back and flew right to it. "What in the...?"

"Do you mind?" a female voice cracked at him.

"Why yes, I do. This is my nest." Cedric was clearly irritated.

"I don't see your name anywhere." The female egret, Bertha, was standing up now. She had her wingtips prominently at her sides as she stood her ground.

"It's right here!" Cedric pointed to where his feet had scratched lines on the outside of the nest.

"You have horrible penmanship. Who in their right mind could read such chicken scratch!" Bertha stuck her beak in the air with her final snub.

"Chicken scratch?! Why I oughta...." Cedric tried to push her out of his nest, but Bertha refused to budge. "Get out!"

"Squatter's rights!" The egret dug her toes into the bottom of the nest.

"Ahhh!" Cedric looked as if he were ready to spit. "You guys go on without me. Clearly, I have to deal with this birdbrain!"

"My brain is much larger than your pea-sized noggin." Bertha let out a huff of air.

"See you, Cedric." Archie waved at him from the ground then put his hand to his mouth. "Run while we still can. I think this will get ugly real fast."

Thunder chuckled as they started to walk away. He lowered his head to the ground and softly spoke. "I think he might have met his match."

Razor turned and peered over his back, shaking his mane out of his eyes. "I think you're right."

They walked a little further before Thunder spoke again. "So, Riley said head southeast. You all in?"

The three of them looked as if they were choosing their answer carefully. Thunder started to feel slightly concerned. It was not that he was incapable of making the journey on his own. He just wanted to have his family there with him. This rag tag bunch of animals was his family: a lion, genet, black banded lizard, three egrets, and a grey African parrot. They were a strange mixture of creatures, but to Thunder they were perfect.

"Unless you don't want to...." Thunder was afraid of the answers. He looked from Dash to his offspring. Maybe he would not want to take the young ones so far away from their home.

"Of course, I do! I just have to send a message to the missus that we'll be home later than expected. Excuse me. I have a bird to catch." Dash darted into the bushes.

Thunder lowered his trunk and scooped up Ayo. She patted his trunk politely. "Excuse me, Mr. Thunder, sir. Could you toss me twice as high this time?"

Thunder snorted. "Yes, Miss Ayo."

When Ayo landed on his back, he went to pick up Khari, who held up a paw. He gestured for Thunder to come closer. Thunder knelt down as far as he could, and Khari stood up and whispered in his ear. "Don't tell her, but please don't toss me that high."

Apparently, little Khari did not want his sister to know he was not as brave as she was. Thunder chuckled. "Right, Khari."

Thunder tossed the young kit onto his back.

"Ha, ha, I beat you," Ayo taunted her brother. "I flew like a bird."

Khari frowned. "Did not!"

"Did too."

"You both flew like birds," Thunder said to appease them both.

Archie chuckled. "Kids…gotta love 'em. I've got nothing holding me back, so you can count me in." Archie raced up Razor's fur and climbed onto his back.

"I'm always in, Thunder." Razor grimaced as Archie pulled on his fur too tight. "You want to relax your grip just a bit there, Archie?"

"Oh. Yeah. Sorry." He let Razor's fur slide from his grasp. "Must have been a twitch."

"Great! Off we go then! Dash will catch up to us." Thunder breathed a sigh of relief. If they kept moving, they might find the lagoon in the next day or so. He certainly hoped so! He could not wait to find out what Spiro had to share with them. Thunder yearned to put all the pieces of the puzzle together. Someday soon, he would find Hope Haven and fulfill his destiny.

Chapter 6
Princess Gabriella

In the southeast rainforest, some of the animals were clearly up to some hijinks. Thunder could hear a ruckus of some kind kicking up nearby. He turned to his friends. "What do you suppose that is?"

"I dunno, but there's only one way to find out. Let's go, shall we?" The small genet raced through the trees followed by Ayo and Khari, who both needed to burn off some energy.

"I think I'll just stay here." Archie gestured to the comfortable post he kept on Razor's back. If his presence ever bothered Razor, the lion never complained.

"Let's go check it out." Thunder followed after Dash. When he reached the animals causing the sounds, he was surprised to see a group of four brush-tailed porcupines and one mongoose.

"What do you suppose they are up to?" Dash was just below Thunder's feet now. Ayo and Khari were standing right by him. They peered around Thunder's feet to see what was happening too.

"No idea." Thunder watched the creatures before him in astonishment.

The mongoose was doing a slow dance with his body. He contorted left and right as if he were hypnotizing a dangerous cobra. He paid no attention to anyone else around him, so caught up in the moment was he. Two of the porcupines lowered their bodies to the ground, and their quills raised high into the air.

Thunder was confused. They looked as if they were about to launch their quills at the mongoose, but porcupines could not shoot their quills. That was ridiculous, right? "They're not about to shoot him, are they?"

"Nah. They can't do that. That's not how those quills work," whispered Razor.

The other two smaller porcupines leapt onto their backs. In a flurry of action, the two on top started to move their feet furiously over the back of the porcupines. Quills launched into the air. The rapid-fire quills shot toward the mongoose, who dodged them easily with his carefree cobra dance. His hand moved up and down, catching a few in mid-air.

At first, Thunder found this quite entertaining, until he realized the quills were missing the mongoose and sailing right over the leaves. He felt one hit between his eyes, a few on his ears and his trunk. "Ouch!"

The porcupines stopped mid-assault and turned to where Thunder and his friends were standing. "Oh dear me! So sorry about that. We didn't see you there."

Archie pushed out of Razor's mane and twanged a quill that had embedded itself into his neck. "Phew! That was close."

Thunder turned to look at Razor and found his friend was covered in quills. He looked like acupuncture gone wrong. Thunder could not help the laugh that built deep within him. As the first one left his mouth, the quills on his trunk shifted and one landed in his mouth. He choked on it for a moment and spit it out. "Yuck!"

Dash glanced up at both of them and started to roll on the ground. He laughed so hard tears were coming out of his eyes. "Oh my gosh! You both look...ha ha ha...I just can't even."

Razor shook his mane out. Archie held on tight as his body flailed through the air. Quills shot outward and a few of them landed right on Dash's backside. The genet yelped and jumped into the air. "Nuts! Watch it, will ya?"

The kits were rolling on the ground in a loud burst of giggles. "Did you see that, Ayo?"

"Yeah, Khari. That was hilarious." Ayo walked over to her father and started to pull the quills from his fur. "Sorry, Papa. But it was funny."

"I suppose it was...," he chuckled.

Thunder coughed and sputtered as laughing spasms hit him. The porcupines looked at the intruders as if they were out of their minds. One of them tilted his head and arched his right eyebrow. "You okay there?"

"Besides being a pin cushion, I think I'm all right." Razor answered first.

When Thunder had stopped laughing, he cleared his throat. "Yeah. Good. What were you doing?"

The mongoose leapt forward and gave them a low bow.

"Well, these guys here bet me that they could hit me, and I told them there was no way they could hit the far side of a barn." He gestured to Thunder. "Looks like we were both kind of right. Uhm…I mean to say…well…."

Dash rolled on the floor laughing again. "Oh, this guy! Ah haahaha. He just called you a barn, Thunder."

"What's a barn?" Khari asked.

"It's something really wide," Razor answered for her. He had a big grin on his face.

Thunder rolled his eyes. It was not the first time someone had commented on his size. Even though he was a pygmy elephant, which was shorter than other elephants, he was still fairly large compared to other animals. The mongoose had the decency to look away from him. Thunder finally let him off the hook. "I get that a lot, actually. No worries. Can someone help me get these off?"

"Oh, let me!" Archie slid off Razor and grabbed on to Thunder's trunk. He climbed up it and started to remove the offending quills.

"Thanks!" Thunder breathed a sigh of relief. His skin was throbbing from the tiny pricks, but he would be fine. "Well, as much as I would like to see a rematch, we have a schedule to keep. It was nice to meet you."

"Right, of course," the mongoose nodded to them. "Again, we're so sorry, right guys?"

A chorus of agreement followed. As Thunder and the others walked away from the curious cluster of animals, he heard a few of them talking about how close they had come to being lunch. They were afraid of Razor, and Thunder did not blame them. He was still a predator after all, even if he still had trouble hunting with his injuries. The poachers that had hurt Razor years ago had left an injury that would bother him for the rest of his life. He was a little malnourished compared to other lions, but he continued to survive nonetheless.

"Well that was...." Archie could not think of the right word to finish his thought.

"Something." Dash chuckled again. "I doubt I'll see anything like that again in this lifetime."

"Who knew a mongoose was that flexible? Did you see the way he contorted his body and the quills flew over his head? That takes some kind of skill." Archie was clearly impressed.

"That's true. I know I could never move that way." Thunder moved his body from left to right and bumped into a tree branch on the way. He raised his trunk up and rubbed his head where the branch struck.

Razor shook his head and rolled his eyes. "I think I've had enough craziness for one day."

A loud screech echoed around from the ground beneath them. Thunder looked down then back up to Razor. "I think you spoke too soon."

The kits looked up at Thunder in fear. He understood at once. He lifted them onto his back and ruffled their fur reassuringly.

Razor smirked at him. "Perhaps. Hello?"

"Hello up there?" the voice was a little high pitched. It came from a crack in the ground below them.

"Yes?" Thunder lowered his head and peered down into the small crack. The ground was not the dirt they had been walking on moments before. Thunder followed the crack and found it attached to a small cave opening a little further away. "Are you stuck inside a cave?"

"Yes! My name is Gabriella. I can't seem to get out." The voice seemed almost tearful. "They just left me here."

"Hi, Gabriella. I'm Thunder. We'll see what we can do." Thunder looked around at the others. "Do you see a larger hole?"

"I'm on it." Dash sniffed along the crack, and when he found a larger opening he shouted, "Here!"

Thunder walked to where Dash had stopped. Sure enough, there was an opening wide enough for a larger animal to get through. "Hmm…well, if we directed Gabriella backwards maybe we can find a way to pull her up."

"Right. You stay there." Razor peered down into the darkness. "Gabriella?"

"Yes?" Her reply was slightly muffled.

"Can you back yourself up a little ways? There's an opening about twenty feet behind you that we think we can pull you up from. Just follow the sound of my voice, okay?" Razor called down.

"Okay. Got it," Gabriella answered him.

For the next few minutes, Razor guided her back to where Thunder stood waiting for her. He had grabbed a vine in hopes that they could slide it down into the hole and pull her up. Thunder lowered the vine. "Grab on, Gabriella."

"Okay!" Her voice was even more muffled as she grabbed onto the vine.

Thunder pulled the vine slowly, backing up a few steps as

he did. He hoped it did not snap before they retrieved Gabriella. Thankfully the vine held. Before he knew it, Thunder found himself staring at the orange snout of a strange crocodile. She squinted a little in the bright sun light, but she did not let go of the vine. Thunder pulled her out a little more and her body squirmed on the ground slightly.

"Wow, would you look at that?" Archie seemed impressed.

"Sorry, what?" Gabriella looked around to see if she could find what was so amazing.

"You. I've never seen anything like you before." Archie moved closer to her. The black banded lizard was looking over every inch of her orange scaled body.

Gabriella smiled. "Well, of course not. I'm royalty, of course."

"Royalty?" Thunder did not quite believe her, but it was not his place to say so.

"Princess Gabriella the third. I'm sure the other cave dwellers did not mean to leave me. We leave the caves every so often. It's breeding season, you know."

"Oh, I see." Thunder bowed before her. "Pleased to meet you, Princess Gabriella." The others imitated his actions.

"Wow, a real honest to goodness princess?" Ayo was in awe. "You're so beautiful!"

"Aren't you sweet! Thank you for rescuing me. I won't forget it. From this day forth, you will be considered a friend of our kind. I will make it known." Gabriella nodded to each of them. "You can be part of my honorary court."

"Why thank you, Princess." Razor bowed to her again

and turned to wink at the others as if they were part of some grand joke.

"Really?" Ayo jumped up and down on Thunder's back. She got so carried away that she tumbled to the ground. "Oh my! How embarrassing!"

"Goodness, careful little one. If you'll excuse me, I must catch up with the others." Princess Gabriella turned from them and ran as fast as her tiny legs could carry her. Before they knew it, she had disappeared into the rainforest.

"Wow…I think I can officially die today. I have literally seen everything." Dash shook his head ruefully.

"Shush! Haven't you learned your lesson yet?" Archie clamped his fingers over Dash's mouth.

"Ha ha ha! You got that right," Razor chuckled beside them.

Thunder smiled. Today was certainly entertaining. Now all they had to do was find the Crystal Lagoon. "Let's keep moving, shall we?"

Chapter 7
Crocodile Rocks

The six of them continued on their way, trying to pretend that nothing bizarre had just happened. Not that it was every day they met royalty, but there was absolutely no way to prove her claims. Thunder decided it was far better to believe it could happen than to bet against it. After all, who would have thought a lion, elephant, genet, and lizard would be the best of friends?

As the time ticked away, Thunder was starting to feel anxious. He was desperate to find any key to the mystery of Hope Haven. Thunder knew his mother would not have sent him in that direction if it was not truly part of his destiny. Thunder sighed. Having a destiny could be a gift and a curse.

From the moment of his birth Thunder had been destined to bring man and beast together, but so far he had only done a little to move them in that direction. When he had saved Imani from drowning, it had encouraged the villagers to treat the elephants with more reverence. This had turned their relationship into one of mutual respect. The relationship was not infallible though. There were still plenty of uprights who didn't protect the animals of the world. In fact, the only value they found was the profit they could make from the harvested animal parts.

Thunder tried to shake those thoughts from his head. He refused to give in to those images. From his early life he had already had more than enough experience with poaching. So had Razor.

"Is it just me, or did it get awfully quiet?" Archie was peering at the rainforest around them. "I mean, no birds, nothing."

Thunder stopped in his tracks. "You know what, you're right."

"That's odd. Maybe it's me?" Razor scanned the trees above him.

"Sometimes you have that effect on people. That's true, but this is different." Dash sniffed the air. "I smell something funky."

Thunder put his feet hard on the ground. The sensitive pads could detect the sound waves caused by movement. He closed his eyes and focused. "Lots of movement. Quiet, as if we're being stalked by something. A lot of somethings...."

Archie gripped Razor's mane tight. "I don't like the sound of that."

"Me either." Dash braced himself for whatever was racing through the forest. He looked far into the distance as he gripped his children to him tightly. "Hyenas!"

Thunder sighed and hung his head in annoyance. "Again? When will they learn?"

The four of them turned to face their attackers. Each of them were ready to take on the clan of hyenas that had been chasing them for the last few years. Within moments the four bolted through the undergrowth, but no one expected the others that crept up behind them.

Delphi sneered at them. "Surprise! Looks like we're late to the party, but we brought some friends."

"Yeah...lots of friends," Jack interjected. He had the decency to cringe when his mother shot him an angry glare.

"So, we gonna do this, or what?" Dash asked the others.

"I'd say or what...." Archie pointed to the hyenas that were coming from the other sides.

The four friends were completely surrounded. There were only two choices; they could stay and fight to the death, or they could run. Since Thunder was not ready to see his friends die, he shouted "Run!!!"

Razor did not wait...he sprang into action. Quickly he grabbed the kits from the ground and held onto them in his mouth. They dangled fearfully from his mouth as he raced forward. Dash ran at his side, his eyes wide with fear for his children.

Thunder lifted his legs and stomped as hard as he could. He startled the first wave of hyenas long enough for his friends to put a little distance between them. Then Thunder turned and raced after them. As hyenas bit at his legs, he kicked them away. Swinging his tusks around, he flung a few far away from him. One of the hyenas hit the tree and yelped. The other was still in air. Thunder did not stay to see how many more were following them.

They made it to the banks of a river that the adults recognized. Dash pointed at the river. "Crocodile Rocks!"

Several "rocks" could be seen from the water. While some animals might have been fooled, these travelers knew better. Those rocks were actually the tops of crocodile heads that were almost always lurking there to eat unsuspecting animals that tried to cross over the river.

"What do we do, Thunder?" Even Razor was looking to him for the answer.

"Well...." Thunder looked at the snarling hyenas that were coming even closer to them. "I say take our chances in the water. Climb on, kids."

Ayo and Khari quickly climbed on top of Thunder's back. They had had very few dealings with larger predators in the past and were beyond terrified.

Delphi heard his answer and started to laugh hysterically. "Looks like the water's going red tonight."

Thunder shivered at the idea of crossing into the dangerous water, but they had no choice. He refused to give his life to any of those vile hyenas. He backed into the river, his head held high as he met Delphi's eyes. He would not go to his death afraid.

The moment his body was immersed in the water, Thunder felt the swish of scales close to his side, and the genets clinging to him in fear. As the largest animal in the water, he was fairly certain the crocodiles would go for him first. "Keep swimming. You have to make it across!"

Four crocodiles were making their way toward Thunder. He was sure he would be a goner until a familiar voice rang out.

"Halt!" Princess Gabriella commanded.

The crocodiles all rose from the water and turned to see the orange crocodile on the other bank. Whispers of "Princess" made their way across the river. Her head rose like a queen before them. "These are our friends. From this moment forward they will have free passage through any of our waters."

"What about the others?" One of the crocodiles pointed across to the hyenas, who looked as if they had seen a hippo fly through the trees.

"Any enemy of our friends is an enemy of ours. Hyenas make a tasty snack, after all." Princess Gabriella saw the way Delphi looked at her. "If I were you, I'd eat that one first. She's looks a little over ripe."

Thunder did not question it. There was no time for that. He turned to the others. "Swim!"

No one wasted another minute. They made it across to the other bank and stood before Princess Gabriella. Thunder bowed low before her. "Thank you, Princess."

"Any time, Thunder. What are friends for, after all?" She gave him a beaming smile. Her mouth was filled with sharp bright teeth that seemed to glimmer in the sun light. "Carry on, fellas. We got this."

"She is a princess! See, I told you!" Ayo was now beaming ridiculously.

The hyenas on the other bank looked depleted. Delphi shook a paw in the air. "This isn't over, Thunder!"

Thunder refused to take the bait. Delphi was not worth

his time. He had a mission to complete. First, on to the Crystal Lagoon. Then hopefully he would find the way to Hope Haven. His destiny was not going to be extinguished today. He was thankful for that.

CHAPTER 8
THE CRYSTAL LAGOON

No one spoke for a while after their encounter. Thunder was still shaking. They could easily have lost their lives back there. All because he had been given the quest to find Hope Haven. It would have been his fault if his friends had died. Thunder finally broke the silence. "I'm sorry...."

Razor looked perplexed for a moment. "For what?"

"We could have died...." Thunder did not know what else to say.

Dash turned around to face him. "We can die any day, Thunder. That's life. It comes with an expiration date. There is no forever, you know?"

"Yes, but you have a family. What if...?" Thunder could not even finish his thought. He looked at Ayo and Khari who were licking the water from their fur. They appeared to act as if nothing had just happened.

"Thunder. Stop. I'm fairly certain none of us have regrets." Razor pawed the ground absently as if he were trying to find more words.

"I know, buddy. I know. We're all in this together. I just…
well, I don't want my quest to find Hope Haven to keep you
from living your lives." Thunder sighed.

"Did you ever consider that Hope Haven might be our
destinies too, Thunder?" Archie's words were unexpected.

"I didn't know you felt that way." Thunder was taken
back slightly.

"Well, sure. I'd like a higher purpose. A legacy far beyond
myself. Who knows? Maybe Hope Haven will be the start of
something big for us all." Archie smiled and his eyes were
filled with dreams that Thunder understood.

"We're in this 'til the end, Thunder." Razor's face was
filled with chiseled determination.

"Okay then. I guess that's that." Thunder ruffled Razor's
mane with his trunk. He took a few more steps, then stopped.
"Do you see that?"

"Hmmm?" Razor looked up at him.

"No, not me. There! Look! That's the tree! It has to be.
Riley said it would be twice as wide as me." Thunder was
excited to see the tree. This meant that Crystal Lagoon was
just around the corner. After all this time, he might just find
the answers he was looking for.

"You're right! Let's go!" Dash had a little extra hop to his
step as he moved forward. His kits followed after him. They
were always up for a good race.

Thunder wanted to race around the tree, but he did not
know what he would find on the other side. So instead, he
moved slowly around the tree with one eye opened. When
he finally came around the tree, he closed both eyes. Taking a

small breath, he opened his eyes and found the most beautiful scene before him.

A waterfall descended over a group of boulders. The stream of water crashed over it, creating a thin mist of rainbows before it crashed to the lagoon below into white foamy swirls. Thunder was amazed at the beauty. "Wow!"

"Sure is something, isn't it?" Archie whistled.

"Yeah." Even Razor seemed impressed.

"I wonder which of them is Spiro?" Dash asked.

The young ones were chasing a blue butterfly around with hardly a care in the world. Ayo leapt up into the air and tried to catch it, but it moved just out of her reach. She eyed her brother as if sizing him up. Before he knew it, she was climbing up his back. Ayo stood on her hind legs and vaulted off him.

"Hey!" Khari glared at her after his face rebounded against the ground.

She gave him a half-smile. "Sorry, Khari."

Thunder looked at the animals gathering around the edge of the lagoon…flamingos, a few forest buffalo, and some red river hogs. Floating on a small pile of wood was a sitatunga. The others seemed to be watching him closely. "My bet is that one." Thunder pointed to the sitatunga.

"Could be." Dash moved closer to the water's edge and lapped up the liquid. "Wow, that's good water!"

Thunder chuckled. He was not surprised. Clear water usually did taste the best. He moved toward the edge of the lagoon and entered its depths. "I'm going to go find out."

The further Thunder moved in the water, the deeper it

became. Soon, Thunder's feet could not touch the bottom. He was surprised at how buoyant he appeared in the water. The lagoon had an optical effect that Thunder did not understand. From here, he could see all the way to the bottom with little effort, but the bottom was nowhere near his feet, even though it looked as if it were. "Wow. That's kinda cool."

"Greetings, elephant!" the sitatunga called to him. He was munching lazily on a flower from the pile nearby. His body was covered in silver fur only set apart by thin white stripes. From the top of his tiny head two horns spiraled out above him. Two turtles came from underneath him and spouted water into the air in steady streams. They looked like spinning fountains around him.

"Are you Spiro?" Thunder did not waste any time.

"Yes...and you are?" Spiro looked at him curiously. "No, wait, let me guess. Traveling with a lion, a genet, and a lizard. Hmmm...there's only one elephant I know who would do that. You must be Thunder."

"You've heard of me?" Thunder was surprised.

"I hear of everyone and everything. I'm well-schooled on the goings on in the rainforests." Spiro gestured to the air with his hoof.

"Of course." Thunder took water into his trunk and splashed it over his back as he tried to think of what to say next. He might as well jump right into it. "I'm looking for a place called Hope Haven."

"Hope Haven...hmmm." Spiro chewed on another flower as he stroked the bottom of his chin with one of his hooves. "Well, I can tell you what I know, but I have never been there."

"Anything you can tell me would be helpful." Thunder felt his heart beating louder. If Spiro had heard of it, that meant it did exist.

"I ran into a pair of gorillas. Goofy guys, those two, but I digress. These two told me of a place where the uprights protect those of our kind. Unusual, that is...."

"Not so unusual, Spiro. I know a few like that back home." Thunder thought about Imani and her family. He had not seen her in a few years. The last visit he had taken to the farm, she had not been anywhere around. He had wondered what had happened to the girl.

"Ah...well, that's good, I suppose. More often than not, the uprights fall on the other spectrum, in my experience. Ran into a group of poachers not too far from here. Thank goodness they have no idea how to find this place. I was able to outrun them easily."

"Poachers?" Thunder felt his heart sink to his stomach.

"Yeah, a horrible lot of uprights for sure. They're hunting our young to sell them. Lots of parents killed in the process of protecting their offspring. Bloody mess, if you ask me." Spiro shook his head sadly.

"But you mentioned that Hope Haven is filled with uprights that are helping our kind, right?" Thunder tried to turn the topic around. He wanted to know about Hope Haven.

"Yes...that's right. Hope Haven, sanctuary for the sick and abandoned. Those gorillas, what were their names again? Farold and Nevin??" Spiro pursed his lips and squinted his eyes. "No, that can't be right...."

Thunder chuckled aloud. "Could it be Harold and

Neville?"

"Why, yes…I think it might be. Two huge gorillas, for sure."

"And they know where to find Hope Haven?" Thunder was starting to feel excited. These two gorillas were very familiar to Thunder. They had been there the day he was born and followed his life since then. He had seen them often over the years, and he knew exactly where to find them.

"Yes. They like to go to something they call a graduation. It happens a few times a year, if I remember correctly. Some kind of procession of animals. Not that exciting, if you ask me, but they seem quite enthralled with it." Spiro pulled a piece of bark off the sticks beneath him.

"Great! Thank you, Spiro! This is just wonderful." Thunder finally felt as if he was heading in the right direction.

"You're welcome. Enjoy your stay here at Crystal Lagoon. Friends are always welcome here." Spiro nodded at Thunder.

"Thank you. I'm sure we'll return." Thunder turned away from Spiro and started to swim back to his friends. They would rest here for a while before heading out to find Harold and Neville. Thunder could not wait to see the goofy gorillas again. Wherever they were hilarity ensued, for sure.

CHAPTER 9
HOPE HAVEN

The sanctuary was abuzz with life today. Hope Haven was a sanctuary for animals that had been abandoned by their herds or were in need of rehabilitation. The land was lined with fences made from logs and ropes. They were high enough to keep animals in and unwanted predators out. The uprights that ran it were often seen patrolling the outskirts to keep poachers at bay as well.

The large property was filled with mid-size huts woven with sticks and grasses. The smaller animals resided within these as they were rehabilitated. Goats, hogs, and other smaller four legged creatures called these their home. The larger animals were free roaming.

Kumani, a female African pygmy elephant, was surrounded by younger elephant calves. They were enjoying their morning meal at the troughs.

"Oooh...fresh potatoes today!" one of the calves named Yumari shouted.

"Yes, they are good," Kumani agreed. The calves had not

been there too long, a month at the most. Kumani was happy to have their company. Having been there for a few years, Kumani had seen others come and go when they were ready.

"Do you think you'll find a herd this time?" Yumari asked again.

"I sure hope so," Kumani sighed.

"I'm sure you will, Kumani," Babs called over to her. Babs was a rhino who had been there nearly as long as Kumani. "We'll both graduate this time, Kumani."

"If only...." Kumani wanted nothing more than to find her forever herd. Ever since she had lost her herd to poachers years ago, Kumani had been waiting to find another to belong to. This would be her sixth time trying to graduate from Hope Haven. The uprights truly believed that the animals within the sanctuary should have the right to return to their proper places in the wild. Unfortunately, making the right match for each animal was a tricky equation that did not always have the right answer every time.

Kumani often wondered what was wrong with her that no other herd had accepted her. She tried to keep her spirits high, but time was running out. Kumani was old enough to have her own offspring instead of tending to the orphans at Hope Haven. Not that she hated her time here. She had grown quite fond of the little tykes.

Kumani looked across at the other animals around her. The small crash of rhinos near her were munching on some of the grasses below them. Some of the goats of the sanctuary had climbed onto their backs, as was their habit in the early morning hours.

One of the goats, Jerome, hopped from one rhino's back to the other. He must have dug his hoof in a little too hard, for the rhino beneath him complained. "Watch it, will you?! Those things are sharp!"

"Ah Gussy, why are you so grumpy this morning?" Jerome called down to him.

Gus snorted. "What's it to you?"

"Come on, it can't be all that bad." Jerome looked at the world around him. "You live in a veritable paradise."

"Paradise?" Gus huffed. "Stuck with the lot of you?"

"Ah, come on, you know you love me." Jerome adjusted himself on Gus's back and the rhino bucked him off.

"Like a cavity...." Gus turned to face him with a glare.

"Seriously, what's eating you?" Jerome looked concerned.

"Don't mind him. He's in the doghouse with Maude," Selma interjected. "Seems she took a liking to that rhino she saw out there last week. We tried to tell her that he already had a mate, but you know how hard it is to convince that one."

"Well, she's not the only female here, you know. What about Selma here?" Jerome used his antlers to gesture to her.

Gus started laughing for the first time today. His snorts were so loud, he was drawing a fair amount of attention to himself. "Selma...ahh, ha ha ha ha. That's a hoot and a half!"

"Well, I never...." Selma stomped her foot and prepared to charge after him.

"Uhm...Gus...I would stop...." Jerome tried to warn him, but he could not get the words out in time. Selma charged at Gus and rammed into him so hard that Gus flew a few feet into the air."

"Wow, that's not something you see every day," Jerome whistled. He sauntered over to Kumani. "Is it safe over here?"

"Sure. We're just relaxing at the moment." Kumani smiled at the goat.

At that moment, the uprights were rolling a large inflated ball around the ground. Kumani saw the fast flapping ears of the calves around her. "Hmmm...on second thought, you might be safer over there." She pointed to the other side of the courtyard.

"You're probably right." Jerome raced away quickly.

"Oh, it's on!" Yumari called out next to her.

Kumani smiled at her tiny friend. "Yes, it is!"

The elephants raced over to the uprights, whose faces were filled with bright smiles. Their laughter erupted around them as the elephants tried to steal the ball away from them. Imani, one of the younger women, walked over to Kumani and handed her a piece of apple. "Hello, Kumani."

Kumani gently grabbed the apple from her hand and shoved it into her mouth. Imani was her favorite upright. The girl always seemed happy to see her, as if she were reminded of another elephant. Kumani stepped closer to her and allowed Imani to put her head on hers.

"I love you too, Kumani. All right. Go play, girl. It might be your last match with the calves before your graduation. We'll find the right match this time, girl. I promise. Daniel has been scouting the area already." Imani stroked Kumani's head all the way down her trunk, where Kumani tickled her hand by blowing hot air out of her nostrils.

"All right, go play," Imani told her one last time.

Kumani raced toward the playful calves that were kicking the ball around the ground. The ball whipped from one to the other. One of the calves was so excited he tripped over the ball and toppled to the ground in a mass of dirt and skin.

"It's all right, George. Get up!" Kumani called to him. All of the calves were used to rough and tumble play from time to time.

Yumari kicked the ball so hard it took flight. Kumani tried to grab it with her trunk, but it continued to sail over her head. Two young giraffes were standing nearby, their necks stretched out high above their bodies. With enough space between them, they looked much like a goal post.

"Yes!" Yumari cheered. "Touch down!"

The giraffes stopped chewing their leaves, turned to look at them in confusion, and shook their heads. The baby giraffe at their feet went after the ball. He moved it carefully with his tiny legs, juggling it under his body. The ball slid out from under his speckled body and landed right at Kumani's feet.

"Thanks, Taavi!"

"You got it!" his cheerful voice called over to them. His long legs seemed to bow every few steps as he hobbled over to them. Taavi had been adopted by the female giraffes at the sanctuary. He was injured when uprights had tried to poach him from the tower of giraffes. Hardly any of them had survived. Kumani would never understand why humans felt the need to destroy such beauty.

"Looking good today, Taavi," Kumani greeted him.

"Thanks! Imani has been helping me learn to walk better."

Taavi grinned at her. "You'll be leaving soon, right Kumani?"

"Yes, Taavi." Kumani kicked the ball to the calves and walked closer to Taavi.

"You will come back and visit, right?" His face was filled with sadness.

"If I'm able to." She stroked her trunk along his neck and smiled. She would miss Taavi. All of them actually, but Kumani knew there was another world out there waiting for her. Kumani was certainly ready for it.

***

On the other side of the rainforest, the egrets were in mild despair. The night before, uprights had come under the cloak of darkness and snatched several of the animals from their slumber.

"I can't believe this!" Sydney raised her fist in the air. "This is war!!"

"Calm down, Sydney. We can't fly off the handle, you know." Persius tried to soothe his sister.

"Calm down? It's personal, Persius! They got Penelope!"

"What?!" Cedric had just joined them. "Who took Penelope?"

"Those disgusting humans!" Sydney's white face was puffing up with anger. "Those poor babies!"

"They took the babies?" Cedric was clearly confused. "I don't understand. Why would they do that?"

"These poachers wanted their prey intact, Cedric. I heard one of them say something about private dealers. I don't know what that means though." Persius shook his head in disgust.

"What are we going to do about it?" Cedric asked them.

"What do you mean? What can we do?" Persius was angry, but he was already feeling defeated.

"We have to find Thunder. He would know what to do. He's been here before, you know." Sydney's voice was filled with wisdom.

"Who's going to watch the kids? Molly is away for a while, doing whatever it is she does when she flies off." Persius crossed his wings in front of him and tapped his feet.

"Frederick can do it," suggested Cedric.

"That batty flamingo? What does he know about watching children?" Persius was not quite on board with it.

"Well, Bertha can too. Maybe they both can. I don't know. All I know is our friend is in trouble and she needs us." Cedric stomped his foot.

"Fine. You get Bertha. I'll find Frederick. Between the two of them we should have this covered." Sydney did not even wait for confirmation. She flew off into the air and headed toward Frederick's lagoon.

"I still can't believe you managed to hook that one, Cedric. That egrets a keeper," teased Persius.

"Well, she wouldn't leave. So I had no choice, I suppose." Cedric gave him a rueful smile.

"Right. Well, you go get her, and then we will use our contacts in the trees to figure out where Thunder and Razor are. We'll find a way to save Penelope and her kids."

"Roger that. I'll be back here before you know it. Keep an eye out for more of those uprights." Cedric saluted his brother and took off into the air.

CHAPTER 10
WILD RACE

Thunder and his small entourage had been traveling for hours. They had stopped long enough to eat, but they were on a mission to find the gorillas. Now that they were near their stomping grounds, Thunder was starting to feel a little more comfortable with their pace.

"Did you hear that?" Dash asked curiously.

"What?" Thunder sometimes thought Dash heard things that did not exist. Thunder put his foot down hard on the ground to see if he could hear any rumblings.

"See?" Dash must have known Thunder felt something.

"Sounds like something big." Thunder wondered if it were more elephants. He thought most of the herds were away from this area. And even if it were elephants, there could not have been more than a few of them.

"Let's go check it out." Dash was already sprinting toward the sounds. The kits followed after him fearlessly.

"You think he has a death wish?" Archie shook his head back and forth. "That one runs without thinking."

Razor chuckled. "That's true."

"Better him than us." Archie moved to the top of Razor's head to get a better view. "What are the odds that he survives this?"

"Pretty good, I would say. He's already found the gorillas. Although I think the kits found them first." Thunder could now see them from here. Ayo was already trying to climb up Neville's back. The gorilla turned and smiled at her before lifting her up onto his shoulder. Khari seemed a little put out until Neville let him climb up too.

Neville and Harold were standing next to a family of rhinos. Thunder wondered what they were up to, as the youngest one seemed to be giggling uncontrollably.

As Thunder approached the silverback gorillas, Neville called to him. "Good day, Thunder."

"Hello, Neville." Thunder gave a half-hearted wave to him, and nodded to Harold too.

"What brings you here to our plains, Thunder?" Harold turned to address him. Thunder realized now why the baby rhino had been so entertained. Harold was wearing different fruit on each of his fingertips. He had been doing a small puppet show for the little tyke. The genets were laughing now too.

"Actually, I was hoping you could tell me where I could find Hope Haven." Thunder felt an extra skip in his heartbeat as he waited for his answer.

"Actually, Thunder, you came at just the right time. For two reasons actually. One, to help us with our race, and two, to find the answer." Neville's smile lit up his face.

"What race?" Dash was already intrigued. If ever there were a time or place to show off his speed, Dash was always up for the challenge.

"Oy! Did you have to mention race? Now we'll never hear the end of it." Archie slapped his head with the palm of his hand. The kits had also heard the word plain as day, and were hopping up and down on Neville's head anxiously.

"Yes, race. We were about to climb on top the rhinos and race across the plains, but we could up the ante a bit." Harold stroked his chin with his fingers.

"Hey, what about Thunder? I mean, you could ride Salem here, Harold. If Thunder gave me a good hoist, I could ride his back. The genet can ride on Obasi's back. The lizard on Razor. We could have a grand ol' race." Neville was clearly proud of himself. It was as if a light bulb was flashing over his head.

"Uh…ride on my back?" Thunder thought Neville might have lost his mind. He might fit on his back, but silverback gorillas were quite large. Thunder could carry him, but more than likely it would not be very fast.

"And what about us?" Ayo was looking up at them curiously.

"Why don't you race down to the finish line with Adisa? You can tell us who wins," suggested Harold.

"Okay!" Ayo and Khari did not waist a moment. They raced over to Adisa and waited for her to find the finish line.

"Yeah. Care to give it shot?" Harold was clearly liking Neville's suggestion.

Thunder looked at both of the gorillas. He did not have

the heart to say no. "Well, I'm game if the rest of them are."

"Game on!" Archie answered for Razor and himself. "We got this, pal!"

"Right...." Razor grimaced a little as he shifted his hip.

The animals got ready. Neville grabbed onto Thunder's trunk and swung up onto his back. The female rhino ran further down the plains to see who the victor was. "On your mark, get set, go!!!"

A mad dash of animals raced across the plains. The ground trembled beneath them as each pair tried to make it there first. If anyone was watching they would have thought they had lost their minds. Only uprights were known to ride animals like this.

"Yahoooo!" screamed Neville. He patted Thunder's side and dug his feet into him. "Let's go, Thunder! Wooohoooo!"

Thunder chuckled. He had to admit this was a lot more fun than it had sounded at first. It was no shocker that Dash and his ride made it to the other side first. The mounts were all catching their breaths when they stopped.

"Wow, that was fun!" cheered Obasi.

"So...uh...so...." Thunder was trying hard to get air in his lungs. "Who are all these rhinos?"

"Oh, this is Salem and his family. In fact, he's the person you came to talk to," Harold answered.

"Oh?" Thunder was confused. He was sure that the gorillas would be the ones that had the answer.

Salem nodded to Thunder. "I'm Salem. This is my mate Adisa and our son Obasi."

"Pleased to meet you." Thunder bowed before them.

"You were asking about Hope Haven?" Salem asked him.

"Yes. I'm on a mission to find it. Do you know where it is and what it is?" Thunder felt like the answers were just beneath the surface now.

"Yes. I know where Hope Haven is. I lived there." Salem seemed to have a sad smile on his face. As he continued his story, Thunder started to understand. "When I was younger, no older than Obasi here, upright poachers came and destroyed my entire life. I was separated from my mother, Soma, and left to fend for myself."

"Wait...." Thunder's breath caught in his chest. "Did you say, Soma?"

"Yes. My mother. I don't know what happened to her. I looked everywhere, but I could not find her." It was clear that even now, the loss of his mother effected Salem.

Thunder could certainly relate, having lost his mother just a few years ago. The thing that caught Thunder off guard was that Soma had been a friend of his. "Salem, I wish...well... Soma did survive the poachers."

"She's alive?" Salem's face lit up.

Thunder hated the fact that he knew his next words would take away the rest of his hope. "She was alive...Soma died. She was a remarkable rhino, Salem. Soma saved my life when the poachers came."

"She was a fierce protector." Salem looked down to the ground. "I barely got to know her before the uprights tore us apart. But they are not all bad."

"That's what I've been trying to tell others. I know a few that are on our side too," Thunder agreed.

"The ones at Hope Haven, they are the best kind. They gave me a safe place, and when I was old enough to find my own way, they set me free. I found Adisa here…well, the rest is history." Salem nodded to his family.

"You have a beautiful family. Is there any way you can tell me where to find Hope Haven?" Thunder felt a small excitement building inside him. He was finally going to find out where his path would take him.

"Tell you, my dear boy. Salem can show you! In fact, we were already heading there." Neville patted Thunder on his back before sliding off him.

"There's going to be another graduation in the next few days. You're welcome to come with us," offered Salem.

"That would be wonderful. Thank you!" Thunder's excitement was palpable. His destiny was just a short journey away. He could not wait to see what would happen next.

***

Across the rainforest, Delphi and her clan were making their own calculated plans. The night before they had heard the uprights creeping through the trees. Delphi had watched them taking birds from their nests.

"Tara!" Delphi called out.

"Yes, Mother?" Tara darted to her side.

"Have you followed the uprights?" Delphi asked her.

"Yes. I followed them through the forest last night. They mostly seemed to take hatchlings from the parrots. I heard them say something about baby elephants on the way out of the forest," Tara reported.

"Elephants?" Delphi felt her stomach grumble at the

thought of them. "You know what this means, right?"

"Ugh...that they might try to capture elephants?" Jack asked. His words were more question than statement.

"Yes, and where there are poachers there is meat. We'll follow after them. First, we'll send our decoy. Where's that leopard?" Delphi turned to look around her. "Leopold?"

Leopold grimaced when he heard his name. For the past few years, he had become accustomed to Delphi's orders. By now, he was getting tired of her dictatorship and the fact that she likened him to some kind of chew toy for the young hyena cubs. He winced as one of the cubs ripped through his ear. "I really hate this job."

He pushed the cubs away and stood up. Walking over to Delphi, he nodded his head in her direction. "Yes, Delphi?"

"You're to go find the uprights. First bait, so to speak. If they go for your skin, we'll know exactly what we're up against." Her orders were crisp and cold.

"You want me to put my life on the line just to see if the uprights are doing what exactly?" Leopold did not like where this was going.

"Harvesting or gathering...." She gave him a wicked smile.

"And if I say no?" Leopold glared at her.

Delphi snapped her teeth together and her four oldest offspring came forward with snarling faces. Their teeth were so sharp, Leopold could see the sun glinting off them. "Fine. I'll go."

Leopold sprung away from the hyenas and started his race across the forest. The more distance he could put between himself and those mangy beasts the better. If he were lucky, maybe the uprights would actually do him in. It would be much better than living an existence under Delphi's rule any longer.

"Give him a day, then follow after him. We'll have our answers before long." Delphi gave a bitter laugh.

"Yes, Mother." Tara started to laugh with her mother. Before long, the whole clan was filled with hysterical guffaws.

CHAPTER 11
GRADUATION

The group had been traveling for most of the day. They had decided to stop and gather food before they continued on. Razor, Dash, and the kits were off hunting for a bite to eat. Thunder dug at the ground with his tusks and brought a few roots up for them to munch on. He offered the first one to Obasi. "Here you go, little guy."

"Thank you, Thunder." Obasi walked over to him and sniffed the food tentatively. When he found the food to his liking, it quickly disappeared. Obasi looked up at Thunder with a curious look on his face. "Why do they call you Thunder?"

"Obasi! Don't be rude," admonished Adisa.

"Not at all. I don't mind answering. When I was born, a large storm filled the sky. The thunder was so loud that my mother felt it was a sign." Thunder smiled at Obasi. "It's actually quite fitting. Watch this...."

Thunder stomped on the ground with his legs, alternating movements. He continued to do until dust kicked up around them. The earth below rumbled beneath his legs. Thunder continued to stomp and Obasi's eyes were wide open.

"You made thunder, Thunder! Wow…that's so awesome!" Obasi was clearly impressed.

Adisa came close to her son and nuzzled him gently with her nose. "Did you say thank you? Mind your manners now, Obasi."

"Thank you, Thunder." Obasi smiled up at him.

"You're welcome, Obasi. You can make little thunder too. All you have to do is stomp your feet."

For the next few minutes, Thunder and Obasi practiced making tiny tremors on the ground. Thunder was reminded how much he would like a family of his own the longer he spent with the tyke. Someday, maybe he would find the perfect mate to start a family with. When Adisa called on her son to rest, Thunder moved closer to Salem, as Razor had taken off to hunt for some food.

"Thank you for spending time with Obasi." Salem pulled some grass up from the ground and continued to munch.

"You're welcome. He's a great kid. You're lucky to have him." Thunder was still feeling slightly nostalgic. "Soma would have been proud of you, Salem."

"I wish I had gotten the chance to know her. How long have you been without your mother, Thunder?" Salem asked him knowingly.

"A few years now. I lost her to a stampede. I would have lost her a lot sooner had Soma not helped me find my home," Thunder explained.

"Why did she not come for me?" Salem's question was

from a deep root of sadness.

Thunder wished he had the right answer, but the truth was Soma was very much an enigma. If the egrets were here, they would have probably had a better chance of explaining it. "As far as I knew, Soma thought her family was dead."

Salem sighed. "I can see that. There was quite a bit of death and destruction when the uprights hit us. Many of us were injured or worse." Salem turned to show the long gash on his side.

"I didn't realize...." Thunder had no words really. When the rhino had explained it earlier, he had thought Salem had just been lost roaming on his own, not that he had been an injured calf.

"The uprights, the ones that took me in, were good people. Hope Haven was like a new home for me. Until I was ready to be on my own." Salem ripped a few more strands of grass up as if lost in thought.

"I'm looking forward to seeing it." Thunder pulled some grass for himself and ate it thoughtfully. Hopefully they would be on their way soon. Thunder was ready to see what part of his destiny Hope Haven would become.

"We're not that far from it. Once we finished here, we'll be there before you know it." Gone was the sadness of moments before when Salem turned to him. "I choose to live without regrets, Thunder. Every life has a cycle. Look what mine has brought me."

Thunder looked over at Adisa and Obasi. Salem was right. Life was filled with many twists and turns. He could consider himself fortunate to find a happiness like the rhinos had. "You're very fortunate."

"Yes...yes I am." Salem smiled.

Thunder ate the remainder of his food in silence. When Razor and the others returned, they were ready to go. Thunder could not wait to get moving. Hope Haven was just around the corner...he could feel it.

When they finally reached their destination, Thunder was surprised. Their group was not the only group of animals that had come for graduation day. While they all kept their distance, several animals had lined the plains. Thunder could not believe it.

"All these animals...." His voice was filled with awe.

"Yes. Every time, too." Neville sat next to him.

"It's truly a beautiful thing," agreed Harold. "We never miss it."

"How is it that the rest of the world doesn't know?" Razor too, seemed in awe of the presence.

"That's the thing with hope. Everyone wants it, but no one wants to share it. Not if it could ruin it." Salem's voice was slightly bitter.

"What do you mean, ruin it?" Thunder asked him.

"How many predators do you see out there?" Salem gestured to the animals with his horn.

"Well...." This time Thunder caught on. None of the animals were predators. He now understood. "They are keeping them safe."

"Yes. Uprights and animals alike, working together in a way no one ever expected." Salem dug at the ground with his left hoof.

Thunder looked past the animals, where the fences of Hope Haven divided the rest of their world from the sanctuary. The fences were fashioned of large logs and ropes. They were not really enough to keep an animal in if they wanted to leave. That meant the animals inside felt safe with their surroundings. That spoke volumes of how well the uprights cared for the animals.

He could see a few rhinos grazing near the fences. Giraffes were feeding from the trees. Elephant calves were in the middle of Hope Haven pushing around some wooden barrels. Thunder smiled as he imagined the tiny trumpeting giggles that must be echoing around them. It had been quite some time since he had heard the sound of a friendly trumpet. Bachelor life had kept him far away from the herds, which was why Thunder had not found a mate.

"I wonder who is coming out today," Obasi whispered.

"Let's take a guess, shall we?" Salem answered him.

"Maybe a rhino?" Obasi watched the animals near the fences. "But they don't seem to be moving."

"Good eyes, Obasi," Thunder commended him. He, too, was now trying to figure out which animal might be coming out today.

"The giraffes are still young, and that little one looks like he still needs some help." Obasi pointed to the smaller giraffe who had a limp.

Thunder could not help thinking how the injured giraffe reminded him of Razor. Thunder wondered if Razor had gotten help if he would have recovered better from his injuries. It would have made the lion's life much easier, but somehow

Thunder knew it would take a lot more than watching an animal be released to make him feel better about the uprights that had turned his world upside down. "He is a lot like you."

Razor must have known where Thunder's thoughts where. He moved closer to him and nodded. "He's strong, though."

"Look! It's an elephant!" Obasi was clearly excited.

"We got one of those already...." Khari sounded a little disappointed.

"Awe, but she's cute!" Ayo disagreed with her brother.

"If you say so. They all look wrinkly to me...no offense, Thunder," Khari complained.

Thunder smirked. "None taken, Khari."

Thunder turned his eyes to the female elephant that was being led to the entrance of the sanctuary. From here, Thunder thought she was like an ordinary elephant, really. But the closer she moved to the fence line, he found himself unable to turn away. Even when the others started to talk about the elephant herd moving toward her, Thunder only had eyes for the elephant cow.

"Look! Here they come! Oh, I do hope she makes it this time!" Adisa was quite caught up in the moment.

"This time?" Thunder asked her. It was her words that had finally broken his trance.

"Yes. What does it make now, Salem? Four tries?" Adisa answered.

"I believe so. This has to be it for her." His words were sad.

"Why?" Thunder was almost afraid of the answer.

"Well, each time they try to pair animals up with their herd or forever family. They have to find the right one. This cow here, I think her name is Kumani, she has had a rough go of it. Her original herd was poached when she was just a calf. She barely made it herself. It's not always easy to find a herd willing to work through abandonment issues."

"Abandonment issues?" Thunder knew that being alone could be hard on any animal.

"Yes. Fear of connecting with others because you're afraid of what will happen to them if you get too attached to them," Adisa answered for him. "You've had a fair share of those yourself."

Salem cleared his throat. "Right. I suppose we all have. She's gotten better though. Look. They seem to be taking to her."

Kumani walked slowly out from Hope Haven and trumpeted to the elephants nearby. They were cautious as they approached her. The female elephants circled around her and she disappeared from sight.

Thunder felt his heart catch in his throat. He could barely breathe, just like the others around him. They truly all wanted Kumani to find her forever home. When the elephants started to move away from Hope Haven moments later, Thunder assumed the worst. That was until he saw that Kumani was following after them. She was ushering a few of the calves along, as an aunt might do.

A loud roar of approval erupted around them as the animals rejoiced for Kumani. They were all wishing her a happy life with her new family. Thunder blinked and realized he was the only one not cheering. He was happy for her, and while he had found Hope Haven as predicted, Thunder had found something more…Kumani, for as her name translated, she was his destiny. Thunder knew it from the top of his head down to the sensitive pads of his feet.

Razor nudged his head against Thunder's leg. "Wake up, lover boy."

"What?" He blinked, shook his head, and turned to look at Razor. "How do you…?"

"I've seen that look before, my friend. I know what it means." Razor looked sad.

"Don't worry, no female will ever come between us," Thunder assured him. Even if Thunder could get Kumani's attention, that did not mean he had to leave all his friends behind.

"We shall see." Razor stretched on his hind legs and yawned.

"Well, Thunder, did you find all your answers?" asked Harold.

"Yes. I did." Thunder looked back at Hope Haven and saw a familiar face. It did his heart good to know his favorite upright had found a place to help those of his kind. Imani was clearly a good example of an upright who cared about the world around her. Now that he knew what Hope Haven was, he would spread the word wherever he could, so that injured animals or those who had lost their way had a place to restore their faith in the world they lived in. But first, he had to find a way to Kumani's heart.

CHAPTER 12
A NEW HERD

Graduation from Hope Haven had gone much better than Kumani could have wished for. Finally she had found a forever home. The herd had adopted her within its folds as if she had always been part of it.

"Kumani, keep an eye on the youngsters," directed Sofie. She was the matriarch of the herd. There were a few other matrons in the herd as well, and Kumani was the only female adult elephant with no calf of her own. Having Kumani work with the calves was part of her preparation for the next stage of her life.

Kumani moved closer to the calves. They moved closer to her, as she knew they would. Kumani had always been good with younger animals. "Come on you guys. Time to get some food."

Timm wrinkled his trunk at her. "Do we have to? I'm not hungry."

"Yes, Timm. We have to eat. If you don't eat, your stomach

will hurt." Kumani ran her trunk over his head and chuckled as he pulled away.

"Well, I could eat a horse!" Tamm interjected.

"A horse? We're vegetarians, not barbarians!" Serena snorted at Tamm. "Tell him, Kumani."

Kumani cleared her throat as she tried to stifle the laughter that was bubbling up from her chest. "Tamm, we don't eat horses."

"What about lions?" Tamm asked curiously.

"We don't eat lions either." Timm shook his head.

"No, silly. Do lions eat horses?" Tamm stuck his tongue out at Timm.

"Boys!" complained Serena. She rolled her eyes and made a gagging sound.

"Well, boys are better than stinky girls any day!" Timm picked up a piece of fruit and chucked it at Serena.

"Ouch! Hey! Quit it!" Serena stomped her feet in annoyance.

"Or what? You'll stomp me to death?" Timm tossed a banana at her.

"That's it!" Serena picked up the closest piece of food and chucked it through the air. It hit Tamm smack dab in the middle of his forehead.

"Hey! What did you do that for?" Tamm joined the food fight, and before long the air was filled with laughter as the calves obliterated the food that had been gathered for them.

By the time Kumani got them under control, they were all covered in food, herself included. "Guys! Look what you did!"

The calves looked around them and had the decency to look ashamed. They were quite pathetic looking as they hung their heads low. Their chorus of "Sorry, Kumani!" tugged at her heart strings.

"Right. Well, now you'll be hungry for sure. That's what happens when you play with your food. And you're going to need a bath." She shook her head disapprovingly.

"A bath!" Tamm shivered slightly. "But I hate baths."

"I guess you should have thought of that before you started your food fight. Besides, do you want to attract ants?" Kumani warned him.

"Ants!" Tamm stood up on his back legs and did a crazy dance as if he were looking for tiny crawling insects. "Anything but those!"

Timm was also visibly concerned. His eyes had gone huge as a blank terrified stare plastered his face. Kumani waved her trunk in front of his eyes, but he did not react. "Timm?"

"Bah! Just shove them both in, Kumani. That will wake Timm up." Serena seemed nonplussed by the whole thing. That was until a touch of dust tickled her trunk. She sniffed and in it went. Serena shook her head and sneezed. Her head shook back and forth so fast that she knocked herself backwards. The tiny calf bowled Timm over, who then rolled into Tamm. Tamm fell against the tree behind him and screamed.

"Not the tree! Anything but the tree! It's crawling with them! Run away!"

The calves trampled the ground under them as they raced toward the waterhole, where they would be safe from the imaginary ants in their head.

"Well, that's one way to get them in the water," Kumani giggled to herself.

"Works every time."

Kumani almost jumped out of her skin. "What the...?!"

Thunder winced as Kumani's trunk slapped him in the head. "Ouch!"

"Oh, sorry. I didn't see...wait, why am I apologizing? What are you doing sneaking up on someone like that?" Kumani stomped her foot in agitation. "And who are you?"

"Sorry. I didn't mean to startle you. I guess you couldn't hear me over the stampede?" Thunder gave her a half-smile.

Kumani took a deep breath to calm herself. "Right. Of course. I'm Kumani...and you are?"

Thunder cleared his throat as if a lump had appeared out of nowhere. "Uh hum. I'm Thunder."

"All right, so we know each other now. I have to get back to my duty, if you don't mind." Kumani turned away from him and started off toward the watering hole. When she turned to look at him, she found Thunder was still watching her every move. Kumani turned back around the minute his eyes met hers. She smiled to herself. Yes, life was certainly looking up.

***

As Thunder retreated from his first encounter with Kumani, he thought his insides would burst. She was even more beautiful in person. He was walking on cloud nine, and almost did not see the turtle on the ground before him.

"Oh, pardon me!" Thunder stepped around him.

103

"Someone's got a case of lovesickness," a bonobo chimp called from above.

"Did you see that though? Strike one!" The bonobo swung his hands as if he had a bat in his hand.

"Do you mind?" Thunder grumbled at him.

"No, not at all," the bonobo giggled. "Hey, get back in there. We could use an instant replay."

Thunder pulled on the branch the chimps were standing on. When he let it go the two went sailing through the air. They grabbed onto the branches above them and swung carefree through the air. Before he knew it, large objects were being hurled at him from above. Thunder put his tusks up against the tree and shook it with all his might. The bononbos came tumbling to the rainforest floor.

"Do you see stars?" one of them whispered to the other.

"Yes…rainbow colored ones," his friend answered.

Thunder ignored them and carried on through the forest. "Someday she'll be mine. I just know it. My mother was right. Hope Haven was my destiny."

As Thunder joined his friends, he found the kits were making the most unusual sounds. Loud, guttural gulps that came out even louder from their mouths when they opened them. "What are you doing?"

"Archie was teaching us how to burp. Baaaa oooppppp." Ayo sounded like she swallowed a bull frog.

Khari interrupted them. "That's nothing. Check this out. Thuunnnnnn-daaaaaaaaaaaarrrrrrrrr!"

Ayo almost choked as she breathed in her brother's exhale. Her face turned green and Thunder thought she was about to lose her lunch. "That smelled like rotten eggs! Oh my...ewwwww. Now I lost my appetite."

"Sorry. You know what eggs do to me." Khari gave her a half-smile.

Thunder sighed. "Archie...."

"What? He left me alone with them. What else was I supposed to do to keep them out of trouble? I almost have them belching all our names now," Archie grinned.

"What a proud parent moment that will be when Dash takes them home to their mother," Thunder snickered. He almost wished he could be there to see that.

"So, did you find her?" Razor had just come up behind him.

"I did." Thunder tried to find the words. This was an awkward situation for him, seeing as how Razor had no potential mates at the moment. Thunder had never been on this side of it before.

"How was it?" Razor gave him an encouraging smile.

"She was...nice...." Thunder could not think of the right words to describe her. Everything he ever thought she might be? But how did one know that from a brief meeting like that?

"Well, that's good." Razor looked away. "So you'll be staying here then?"

"For now. You could stay too, if you wanted," Thunder offered.

"I'm in no hurry to leave." Razor plopped down on the ground and yawned loudly.

"Good." Thunder was relieved. It was a lot easier to go through life and all its changes when you had those around that cared about you. He was lucky to have his makeshift family. He had no idea what was going to happen next, but at least he was not alone.

CHAPTER 13
FIRST BLUSH

Ayo and Khari were climbing a tree nearby. Their giggles were nonstop as they made headway up the tree, only to slide down to the bottom. Archie sat nearby, shaking his head at them. "Nah, you gotta really latch onto the bark with your claws. Let me show you."

The lizard leapt at the tree and landed just above their heads. His sharp claws attached to the tree easily. "Now, one foot at a time."

The kits watched him carefully. Ayo turned and whispered to her brother, "Should we warn him about the top?"

"Nah. He'll figure it out soon enough." Khari grinned at her.

Archie continued to climb up the tree with little care. He called down directions again. "See, form is important. A straight back can really help."

"Uh-huh," the kits answered him.

"Now just a little...ah!" Archie's foot got caught in sticky sap. He tried to pull his foot free, but it was almost cemented down. "This is disgusting!"

Ayo giggled loudly. "Now you see why we came back down."

A loud buzzing sound started to fill the air, and Archie was filled with mild panic. "Are those...? Oh no! Bees! Get me down from here! Thunder, help!"

Thunder smirked. He was used to saving the lizard from himself. Thunder latched onto his tail with his trunk and started to pull him free. When Archie's foot finally came free, he flew through the air and landed with a loud smack on a boulder nearby.

"Sorry, Archie!"

"I'm O...kay...." Archie lay flat on his face, but raised one hand up behind him to give a thumb's up sign.

Ayo and Khari raced over to Archie and helped him to stand. Ayo put her head against Archie's. "Sorry, Archie."

"No worries, kid." Archie gave her a half smile.

At this point, Dash returned with fresh food for the kits. "Eat up kids! We have to get this show on the road."

Thunder sighed. He was going to miss the kits. They had made the trip so much more fun. "I wish you could stay."

"Me too, Thunder, but the missus will surely be worrying by now. When do you think you're going to come home?" Dash asked him curiously.

"I don't know, Dash." Thunder looked across the tree line to where Kumani was grazing with her herd.

Dash followed his eyes and saw the female elephant. "She is lovely, Thunder. How's the wooing going?"

"I've spoken to her a few times, but I don't know."

Thunder was not real experienced where it came to females. He thought he saw her smile at him once, but it might have been a fluke.

"Don't give up. The best ones are worth fighting for," Dash encouraged him.

"I'm not giving up yet, Dash. I just have to find the right moment to tell her." Thunder felt his heart lurch into his throat at the thought of telling Kumani how he felt. He shuddered at the thought of sharing his emotions with anyone. Thunder was used to keeping them hidden deep beneath the surface. He had lost so much in his life already that he was afraid to wish for more.

"There won't be a good time if you spend all your time stalking the poor thing," Archie teased him.

"I'm not stalking her, Archie." Thunder sniffed in irritation.

"If your conversation repertoire consists of hi, good morning, nice to see you…it's border line." Archie patted him on the back. "Don't worry. There's always more in the sea. What about that one?"

Thunder looked at the older matron Archie pointed to. "She's old enough to be my mother!"

"I'm kidding you!" Archie chuckled.

"Ah well, kid, you'll win her over. I'm sure of it," encouraged Dash. "Well, enough small talk. I gotta get these kids home. Say goodbye, kids."

The kits raced over to their father. Ayo looked up at Thunder with huge tearful eyes. "Bye, Thunder."

"Awe, Ayo. Don't worry. I'll be home soon." He swept

her up from the ground and cuddled her near his head. "Be good for your papa."

"Yes, Thunder," Ayo nodded at him solemnly.

Thunder put her down on the ground and looked at her brother. "And you, Khari...."

"Yes?" Khari looked up at him expectantly.

"Take care of your family for me, will you? Be brave...." Thunder ruffled his fur with his trunk.

"Yes, I will!" Khari wrapped his paws around his trunk and purred against him.

"Off you go!"

Thunder watched as the genets left. Archie and him sat in silence, a little deflated by their departure, but they did what any guy in their situation would do. They refused to talk about it.

***

Kumani watched Thunder from across the plains. He had more than caught her eye. These days, he was almost all she could think about, which annoyed her. She saw him embracing the tiny genets and was reminded what a great father he would be, but she could not help wondering about the company he kept. "Why is he surrounded by such animals?"

She spoked more to herself than anyone else, considering she was standing there by herself. Kumani realized how crazy she must look. She gave a disgusted snort. "I've gone around the bend. I'm even talking to myself."

"Yes, you are!" Tamm giggled. "Are you okay, Kumani?"

"Yes, Tamm. Just fine." She shook her head and tried to

111

hide her embarrassment.

"You sure? Is it your old age?" His words seemed innocent, but his smile gave away his intent.

"I'm not *that* old! I could still beat you!" Kumani challenged him.

"Oh, it's on!" Tamm did not even wait for Kumani to tell him when to go. His little legs kicked into motion.

The two of them raced across the plains to where the entire herd was grazing. By the time they reached them, Kumani and Tamm were both giggling like little children. Kumani snuggled him against her. "I think it was a tie."

"If you say so," grumbled Tamm. He struggled against her hug at first, but then cuddled against her. "I'm glad you're here, Kumani."

"Me too, Tamm." She felt a tear in the corner of her eye and blinked it away. For the first time in forever, Kumani felt like her life not only had a purpose, but that there might be a future for her too. She turned to look at Thunder once more. He was now tossing one of the kits in the air. He seemed so carefree. Kumani envied that.

Beeza, a matron of the herd, turned to her. "You've caught his eyes."

"Hmm…what?" Kumani pretended to not understand her words.

"That bull out there." Beeza pointed to where Thunder stood.

"So it seems," Kumani blushed.

"Do you know who that is?" Beeza asked her.

"Thunder," she answered her.

"That's Thunder?" Beeza was visibly impressed.

"Yeah....?" Kumani could not figure out why his name was such a big deal.

"Thunder is legendary around here. His destiny was foretold by the Great Tusker in the sky. Thunder has already brought man and beast together. His mother, Serenity, was a strong matron of her herd."

"What happened to her?" Kumani was definitely interested in learning more about him.

"She was the casualty of a stampede." Beeza looked down at the ground sadly.

"What about his father?"

"His father, Caden, died before Thunder was born. Poachers...." Beeza shuddered.

"That's sad. So, Thunder has no family?" Kumani could certainly relate. She had been without her family.

"He is a bachelor who roams the world with an odd assortment of animals. If you are truly interested, he would be a great addition to this herd." Beeza gave her approval.

Kumani felt butterflies fluttering in her chest. One of the reasons she had put Thunder off was that she did not want to lose her home within her new herd. They had been the first place to feel like home. She did not want to lose them. Knowing they would accept Thunder into their fold made her worry less.

Kumani gave Beeza a beaming smile. "He would, wouldn't he?"

Beeza put her head on Kumani's and nuzzled her. "You will always have a home with us, Kumani."

Tears flowed down her face. Kumani did not even bother to stop them. Her heart felt light as she whispered, "Home...."

ERIK DANIEL SHEIN & MELISSA DAVIS

CHAPTER 14
CHANGE OF HEART

The plains were quiet, in a way that made Leopold feel uneasy. He had been following the uprights as directed by Delphi. So far, they had not done much of anything, but Leopold could tell they were ready for something more. From his perch in the tree he heard them talking.

"There's a herd right out there," one of the uprights said. His name was Joseph.

"You know, we could cash in on some of those tusks," suggested another who was sitting against the trunk of a tree. His eyes seemed colder than the others.

"No!" The upright Oscar interrupted. "You may be okay with the death and destruction, Raoul, but I am not paid enough for that."

"What's the difference? We're still breaking the law." Joseph crossed his arms over his chest and propped up against the tree. He was their leader.

"It's worse though, Joseph. And you know it." Oscar refused to look at the others.

"Get ready to move." Joseph ignored him and reached for his gun. "We're just after the calves, Raoul. Oscar, remember to chase them toward the other men."

"Right, boss." Raoul grabbed his gun and prepared to follow his orders.

Leopold was not precisely sure what the uprights were talking about, but he had heard stories about the sticks they carried in their hands. Loud and destructive, these boom sticks had the ability to fell the largest animal out there. His hair stood up on the back of his neck. "Something wicked this way comes...."

Before he knew it, a loud screech filled the air as a small monkey tried to warn the animals around them. The monkey jumped up and down, pointing to the weapons that the uprights carried in their hands. "Run! Run! Run! Here they come!"

The tiny voice was not loud enough to stretch across the plains. Leopold watched helplessly as the men started to shoot their guns into the air. Loud crashing booms obliterated the peaceful evening. Screams of terror echoed in the dark night sky as a massive stampede of animals dashed away from the uprights. The herd of elephants refused to back down as the men approached.

"Oh no...just run!" Leopold tried to shout, but his words barely came out. He watched as the uprights toppled the oldest matriarch. She crashed to the floor in a heap of agonizing screams. Another elephant toppled to the ground.

There was one last young female that tried to protect the three calves from the herd. Her legs raised in the air and

117

she tried to kick them away. The upright called Oscar came from behind her, and when she attempted to charge the other uprights, he slammed the gun down on her head. Her head jerked back and she fell to the ground.

"Get the calves!" the man ordered. His men scrambled into action.

Leopold was stuck there in the tree, too trapped in his fear to respond. He wanted to leap onto the uprights and rip into them with his claws, but Leopold had always been on the opposite side of the fence. His vendetta with the elephants had been long and grueling, but in this moment, he felt nothing but anguish for the destruction he saw before him.

By the time his fear subsided, the uprights were long gone. Leopold leapt from the tree and walked the path of the carnage. It was clear that the first two elephants had lost their lives this night. He bowed before each of them. "I'm sorry."

The third elephant was a different story. When Leopold got closer to her, he could hear her breathing still. Leopold stepped closer. "Hello?

Her moans were the only answer. "Ooooo."

"It's okay. I'm here," Leopold assured her. He knew it would be little consolation, but Leopold refused to leave her side. Of all the bad things he had done in his lifetime, this would be the first step to his redemption. He would make sure the elephant survived, and if possible, he would help find a way to stop the uprights from doing this again. Leopold curled up next to her and tried to soothe her until she regained consciousness.

***

Thunder was asleep in the rainforest when he heard an agonizing scream. It haunted him like a memory from long ago. His eyes fluttered open and panic entered his heart. He recognized that voice. "Kumani!"

Thunder bolted to his feet, which woke the slumbering lion. "Thunder?"

"Did you hear that?" Thunder's face had gone pale as memories of the poachers from his childhood entered his head.

"Was that a gun?" Razor was all too familiar with this weapon. He too was fighting ghosts of his past.

"I think so. And I heard Kumani. We have to go, Razor!" Thunder did not even wait to see if his friend would join him. His legs carried him faster than they ever had. "If something happened to her...."

Razor was keeping pace beside him. "We'll find her, Thunder."

Fight or flight no longer existed for him. He was on autopilot with one thing in mind, saving Kumani no matter the risk. He dodged branches left and right as he raced through the forest. When he broke through the trees, he got his first glimpse of the devastation before him. Animals were stampeding around him, heading away from the chaos. Thunder did not question his need to move toward danger.

As they neared the middle of the plains, Thunder saw two elephants right next to each other. He stopped near them long enough to determine that there was nothing more he could do for them and to verify that neither one of them was Kumani. He continued on and saw his worst fears.

"Kumani!" Thunder's shout echoed across the plain.

Razor tried to stop him from moving forward. "Thunder… wait!"

There was nothing the lion could do to keep him from closing in on her crumpled body. When he saw the leopard near her, he almost lost his mind. "Get away from her, you mangy beast!" Thunder charged at Leopold, who moved out of the way just in time. At this point Thunder was seeing red and was out for blood. "No scavenger is going to take her!"

Thunder was mid charge when a voice called to him. "Thunder…."

He stopped in his tracks and turned to Kumani. "Kumani?"

"I'm fine. Just help me up, will you?" Kumani struggled to get up. She put her trunk to her head. "I think I'm seeing stars…."

Thunder abandoned his attack and raced over to her. He let her steady herself against him. "Are you okay?"

Leopold had crept closer. "Can I help?"

"Go away, you foul creature!" Thunder was still prepared to take the leopard out at any moment.

"Thunder, stop! He was trying to help," Kumani admonished him.

"Leopold? Help? Maybe you did hit your head harder than you thought…." Thunder looked at her as if she had lost her mind.

"It's true, Thunder." Leopold hung his head. "I know I've done some awful things, but I would never wish this…." He gestured to the destruction around them. "On anyone."

"Right…." Thunder still did not believe him.

120

Razor, however, did. "If you mean that, then you have a lot to change."

"Yes, I know. The first thing I want to do is help you find the calves. The rest of the herd went that way." He pointed to the path the terrified elephants had taken. "The uprights went in the opposite direction."

"Right...." Kumani was trying to think. "We can't do this alone. I have an idea."

Thunder looked at her intently. "Anything we can do to help, I'm game."

"We need to return to Hope Haven." Kumani's words fell flat.

"How will that help?" Leopold asked her.

"Because the uprights there will know something is wrong. They will follow us. We can lead them directly to them. If there's one thing I learned from my time at the sanctuary, it's that these poachers are not well liked at all. The people of Hope Haven will protect us." Kumani's words were confident.

Thunder had no problem believing her. He had known one of the uprights since he was a calf. Imani would definitely risk everything to save them. These were the right humans to have on their side. It reminded Thunder of the Great Tusker in the sky who believed that man and beast should work together to make the world a better place. This was his infinite plan.

"Let's do it," Thunder agreed. As soon as Kumani was ready to travel they would make their way to Hope Haven.

Kumani turned to the fallen elephants and walked over

121

to them. Thunder gave her space. He watched as she knelt down next to them, paying the proper respect for their life force that had already left them. Her sad wails filled the air as she allowed herself a few moments to mourn. When she was done, she returned to them with a tear stained face. She did not bother to hide her anguish. "Let's go."

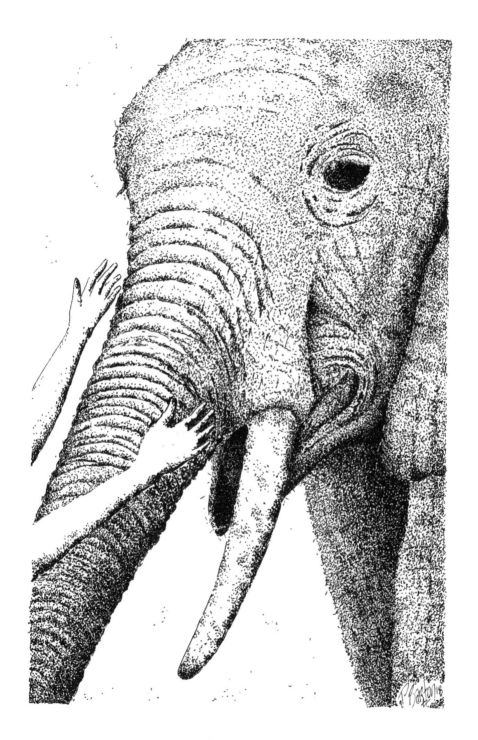

Chapter 15
Seeking Help

Like a beating drum their feet moved across the plains. Lion, leopard, lizard, and elephants all joined together to bring the calves back to the herd. As they started to leave the outskirts of the plains, a few of the herd were returning.

"Where are you going, Kumani?" Beeza asked her.

"To bring our calves back. Are you coming?" Kumani was determined. She paused just enough to fill her in. "Hope Haven is our one chance."

Beeza held her head high as she called to the others. "Today, we fight back. Let's get our calves."

"That's the spirit!" applauded Thunder. Together, they would make a difference. They had to. Giving up was not a choice.

The other elephants trumpeted. Kumani bowed her head to them before turning back to the problem at hand. "Let's move!"

The animals charged across the plains and made their way through the small rainforest that separated them from Hope

Haven. Their hearts beat as one infinite group as they raced forward. No more would they be complacent to poachers that thought very little for the price they paid when they took down Africa's majestic creatures.

Thunder, for the first time in years, felt like part of a herd, even though the circumstances were not of his choosing. He was unsure what the future might bring, but in this moment, he could not focus on that. Watching Kumani's strength and courage only confirmed his feelings for her. He was proud to be at her side.

If any of the animals thought the party of animals was odd, none made any comment. In fact, they were sitting in awestruck silence. "Would you look at that?" a bonobo chimp called out.

"Yeah. You don't see that every day," another one answered.

Tiny land animals scurried out of the way. The dust they kicked up made a few rodents cough and sputter when they stopped to watch the elephants running through their territory. A few shook in fear when they saw the large cats accompanying them, until they realized that the predators were too focused to give them a second thought.

As the elephants neared Hope Haven, Razor started to pull back. "We're going to scout the area, Thunder. Maybe we'll be able to track them from here. We'll meet back up with you soon."

Razor let Archie climb on his back. He turned around to face Thunder one last time. "Happy hunting."

Thunder nodded at him, then turned to Kumani. "Now

what?"

"We get as close to the fence line as we can. Stomp, trumpet, whatever it takes." Kumani looked around to make sure the other elephants understood her.

"You got it, Kumani," Beeza answered her.

The elephants raced to the border of Hope Haven. Thunder stomped as hard as he had ever stomped before, hoping that his movements would be heard by the animals inside. The other elephants called out to the occupants inside, their loud trumpets filling the air like an overpowering orchestra.

The elephant calves nearby stirred from their slumber. Their tiny trumpets filled the air as they returned their calls. The rhinos just past the calves pounded the ground with their hooves. Within moments, a few uprights came racing out of their huts.

"What in the world?" Daniel turned on one of his lamps and carried it around the courtyard. He turned to the sound of the elephants and his eyes peered closer in the darkness around him. "Imani!"

"Yes?" Imani called through the hut near him.

"I think we have a problem. It's Kumani." Daniel headed to the fence. Before he knew it, Imani was on his heels.

Imani called out to her. "You okay, girl?"

Kumani walked closer to her and nuzzled her face affectionately with her trunk. She allowed herself a brief moment of contact with her before she grabbed onto Imani's hand with her trunk. Pulling her forward a few steps, Kumani tried to get her to understand.

"I don't know if she understands you, Kumani." Thunder

walked closer to Imani. "Let me try."

Thunder stepped closer to Imani, and at first she recoiled away from him. After a moment, her eyes adjusted to the darkness and she really looked at him.

"This can't be. Is it you, old boy?" Imani held her hand out and Thunder took it. Imani let her fingers travel up his head, and when she put her head on his, Thunder knew she understood.

"There's trouble, right?" Imani was not really looking for an answer. She turned to Daniel. "We have to follow them. There's something wrong. Bring whoever we have."

"Imani, it's the middle of the night—" Daniel tried to explain.

"Yes. Prime poaching time. Do you remember the elephant I told you about, Daniel?" Imani's eyes were filled with a memory only she could see.

"Yes. The one who saved you from drowning?" Daniel stepped closer to Thunder.

"Yes. Here he is, and if he has come to ask for help, then he will get it. Get everyone."

Thunder could not help but notice that Imani seemed to be in charge. He felt pride through every inch of his body. This was one upright who had defied the plan that others had for her. Instead of promoting the destruction of innocent creatures, Imani had pledged to preserve and protect them. Having a place like Hope Haven was almost like a natural wonder. This sanctuary was everything the Great Tusker in the sky would have wanted.

Turning away from her, Thunder gestured for the others

127

to follow him. "They'll come. We have to find Razor's track. If anyone can find those calves, he can."

Kumani nodded to him. "I believe you, Thunder. Let's find him."

Beeza nodded her agreement. "Off we go."

The elephants did not wait for the uprights to follow. They sought the path to redemption…their future lay with the young calves, as did any other herd. To ensure the survival of their species, they would do whatever it took to protect them. This time, the animals were fighting back.

As they zipped through the trees, Thunder heard a familiar voice. "Thunder!"

"Cedric?" Thunder stopped in his tracks. There was something in his voice that made it clear that something was horribly wrong.

"They have Penelope!" He was gasping for breath as he landed on Thunder's back.

"Who has Penelope?" Thunder felt fear grip his heart.

"Those poachers…they came and took her and her babies." Persius had now arrived on the scene, followed by a very angry Sydney.

"I'm going to kill every single one of them!" Sydney threatened menacingly.

"Stop. Hold up a moment. We are not going to kill anyone. We'd be stooping to their level. We will take back what's ours, though. We're already heading to find them," Thunder tried to explain.

The other two egrets landed on his back. Sydney raised a wing in the air. "We're with you. No one hurts my family!"

At this point, Kumani was now at his side. "You coming?"

"Yes. I just had to pick up my friends. Guys, this is Kumani. Kumani, this is my family." Thunder gave a brief introduction.

"Pleased to meet you. I just wish it were under different circumstances." Kumani nodded to the herd ahead of them. "We need to catch up."

"Right. On we go!"

CHAPTER 16
THE CAMP

When they met up with Razor and Leopold they were racing toward them. Thunder tried to catch his breath. "Uh... did...you...ugh...did you find them?"

"Yes. We did. There is a camp of uprights due east of here. They have the calves corralled in a pen," Leopold answered him.

Razor's nose twitched in anger. "They have Penelope too. Those poor calves are terrified. We wanted to spring them free, but we knew it would be better to wait."

"And the uprights?" Thunder wanted to take stock of the whole situation. They needed an accurate picture painted for them. He did not want them to go in without enough information, plus they were waiting for Imani to catch up to them.

"They seemed to be celebrating when we came upon them. Acting wild and carrying on. I've never seen such a thing...," Leopold answered.

"I have...." Razor could not meet their eyes. "The uprights

that came at me years ago, some of them acted as if they'd had fermented fruit. Their legs collapsed beneath their feet and their eyes were a little crazed. These uprights were acting the same way."

"Well, this could actually be an advantage to us," Kumani weighed in. "If they are distracted, it might be easier to get the animals to safety. We'll wait to see what our uprights do, though."

Thunder turned to the sound of cracking sticks. He saw Imani holding up a hand to tell them it was just her. "Here they are. Let's move on. Lead us to the camp, guys."

Through the dark cover of night, the animals led their humans through the forest until they came to the outskirts of the poachers' camp. A large pen was dead center of the camp. While the calves could probably have broken free from the pen, they were huddled together in fear, trauma making them unable to act. The three calves from Kumani's herd seemed to be surrounding another tiny calf. From here, Thunder could barely see him…he was much smaller than the others.

Cages lined the area, some empty, others filled with reptiles and birds that the poachers would be selling on the black market. This illegal activity was something that had been running rampant in their lands. If it were legal, these uprights would not wait until the cover of night to raid groups of unsuspecting animals.

They took stock of where every upright was located. It would make rescuing their friends easier. There were two tents, with the warm glow of lanterns tracing the silhouettes of the uprights that were snoring loudly from their depths.

"I thought you said they were singing?" Cedric whispered to Razor.

"They were." Razor shrugged his shoulders.

In the middle of the camp was a fire with two uprights sitting next to it. "We need someone to fly near the camp. I can't tell if they're asleep from here," Thunder instructed.

"On it!" Sydney started to fly into the air when Persius grabbed her wing.

"Be careful...." His words may have seemed like just caution, but his eyes reflected a deep concern for her welfare.

"I will." Sydney looked him in the eyes. "Penelope is our family too."

Sydney flew over to the tree just above the camp. She peered down at the uprights to see if there was any sign of active life. When she saw that these uprights were asleep too, she gave a quick jerk of her head.

In the next few moments something strange happened. It was as if animal and man had crossed some kind of language barrier. They spoke in actions, not words. Imani and Daniel put up a hand to Thunder and the other elephants. "Stay here."

Kumani started to move forward, but Thunder put his trunk on her back. "Don't. I think they are going to bring them back to us."

Kumani glared at him. "We need to help—"

"We are. Those little ones trust you. You are going to help lead them back to Hope Haven." Thunder pulled his trunk away quickly and flushed in embarrassment. He probably should not have done that.

133

Kumani gave him a half smile. "Fine. We'll wait."

Imani and Daniel tiptoed through the camp. As they reached the cages, they started to open them one at a time. They did not take much time at each, for these animals were ready to fight for their freedom.

When they reached Penelope's cage, she looked up at them. The latch opened and she hopped onto the door, using it as a perch. Three tiny hatchlings hopped after her. Thunder breathed a sigh of relief when they did so without making a sound. Imani offered an arm and the African grey parrot seemed to understand that she was there to help. Penelope climbed up her arm and stood on her shoulder as Imani reached in and grabbed the hatchlings. She used her shirt as a pouch to keep them safe.

While Imani finished up with the birds, Daniel walked over to where the calves were shaking. He opened the pen wide and walked closer to the trembling youngsters. He shooed them quietly out the gate, and when the three calves moved away, Thunder saw the other calve that had been hidden moments before. He stood there sucking his trunk like a lost child. His skin was not the same rusty color as all the other calves. Instead it was a pale pink with dark splotches. As Daniel stepped closer to him, Thunder could see the calf had trouble tracking his movement with his eyes.

"He can't see," Thunder whispered. At that moment, Thunder did the only thing that made sense. He walked as quietly as he could through the camp, holding his breath as he did so. He was so afraid he would make noise that would wake the sleeping uprights nearby.

As he got near the pen, Daniel moved aside. It was as if they understood each other. Thunder put a trunk on the little calf's head and spoke softly to him with a shuffle of his feet. "I'm Thunder. I'm here to take you to safety."

"I'm Pasha. And thank you." Pasha let go of his trunk long enough to answer him. The small calf was visibly relieved.

"I'm going to put my tail right before you. Just grab on to it and I will help you out of here." Thunder backed up and waited for Pasha to grab onto him. When he did, Thunder eased him quietly from the pen. Making their way around the camp required a little bit of effort on his part. Each step of the way, Thunder worried that the uprights could wake at any time. While they had Imani and Daniel there with them, the two of them would not be enough to keep all the other uprights at bay.

Thankfully, luck was on their side. In a matter of moments, the camp had been cleared of its captive animals. As they made their way back to Hope Haven, no one seemed willing to speak a word. The worst may be over, but there was no need to push their luck any further than they had to.

CHAPTER 17
MISSING ANIMALS

In the early morning hours, Delphi and her clan crept closer to the camp where the poachers were still sleeping. The sun had not even started its climb into the sky. "What happened to all their animals?"

"What do you mean?" asked Jack. His eyes were almost glazed over as his words left his mouth.

"Did you use your tracking skills or were you just out for a merry old stroll?" Tara snapped at her brother.

He shoved her against the shoulder and snapped at her with his teeth. The two of them toppled over each other and landed with a thud at their mother's feet.

"Get up!" she snarled at them.

They both quickly jumped to attention with a few yelps. Simone sniffed at them. "How old are we now?"

"Shut up. It's not my fault you're the favorite," grumbled Tara. She pawed at the ground in an angry huff.

"You make it so easy though...." Simone smiled sweetly at her before shoving Tara's face into the ground.

137

"Oh, look. They're waking." Jack gestured to the camp.

"This will be good," predicted Delphi.

"What do you mean?" asked Tara as she trotted over to her and peered over her shoulder.

"What happened the last time you lost our prey?" Delphi asked her.

"You almost knocked Jack's teeth out." Tara looked over at her brother, who was glaring at her. "Served him right though."

"Right...watch and see." Delphi nodded to the camp.

***

The first upright that came out of the tent was Joseph, the leader of the camp. He started to throw everything in sight when he saw all the animals were missing. His anger only started to climb when he saw footprints much like his own. "Who let them out? Which one of you did it?"

"What? What's wrong, Papa?" A young upright came out of the tent. He looked up at his father's furious face with fear plastered on his own.

"Did you do this, Pal?" Joseph stared down at his son. "I know you did not want to come with us this time."

"No, Papa. I promise." The boy looked away from his father's angry stare.

"Leave him be, Joseph." Oscar came over from the fire that had fizzled out long ago. "Those shoeprints are twice his size."

"Was it you then?" Joseph accused him.

"Why would I do that?" Oscar asked him.

"Because you're an animal lover, like this one." He

138

nodded to his child in disgust.

"I never said I loved them, only that I didn't want to kill them. Besides, how will they make more babies if you kill them all off?" Oscar's logic was sound. They needed the adult elephants to create more babies for them to sell.

Raoul came out of the tent, grabbing his head as if it were threatening to pop off his shoulders. "Why are you fighting?"

"The animals are gone, Raoul," Joseph growled at him.

"So, we'll find more." Raoul shrugged his shoulders as if this were not a major setback.

"Are you daft? We needed those calves." Joseph looked like he was ready to have a coronary...his face was inflated and three shades of red.

"Eh-hem...." Oscar interrupted. "They left tracks."

"So, they did." Raoul knelt down by the set of tracks that was clearly from a larger elephant. "Looks like the herd came to rescue their young. I told you we should have taken them out."

"This time we will." Joseph grabbed two guns. He tossed one into his son's hand. "Be ready to kill, Pal."

Pal looked caught between wanting to please his father and not wanting to end another life, but he took the gun as ordered. "Yes, Papa."

"See, Oscar. Even my kid has more nerve than you." Joseph turned away from them and started to track the footprints left by the elephants.

***

Delphi stood up and paced around in circles for a moment. She was trying to determine what their next move should be.

If they followed the uprights closely, they might be able to get a free meal. But then again, they could easily become the meal. Uprights were not too choosy when it came to putting fresh meat in their bellies.

"What should we do?" Tara asked her mother. Tara really seemed to be at a loss.

When Delphi did not answer, Simone chose to give her input. "I think we should follow them."

"Why?" asked Jack. "Aren't they a little crazy right now?"

"Yes, but where there are crazy uprights, there are loose triggers. It might mean a new meal ticket for us." The way Simone's eyes were glazed over, she was already imagining a fresh meal.

"And if those bullets hit us instead?" Delphi was still not convinced that following the humans would be the right thing to do under these circumstances.

"What if we kept our distance?" suggested Jack.

Delphi looked at her son as if it were the first time he had ever spoken. His words actually made sense for a change. "That could work."

"It has to. Think of all the delicious meat they could already be leaving in their wake." Tara was clearly sold.

Delphi turned to Simone. "Daughter?"

"I think we could be safe enough if we keep a distance. Right now, they don't even know we're here. If they are keeping their eyes forward, chances are they won't even look back to us." Simone nodded to the direction the uprights had started to move in.

"True. All right, follow them we will." Delphi started

to move forward and her children moved to her side. A few other hyenas followed further back a distance, as was their nature. Today, if things went well, they would all be in dining heaven.

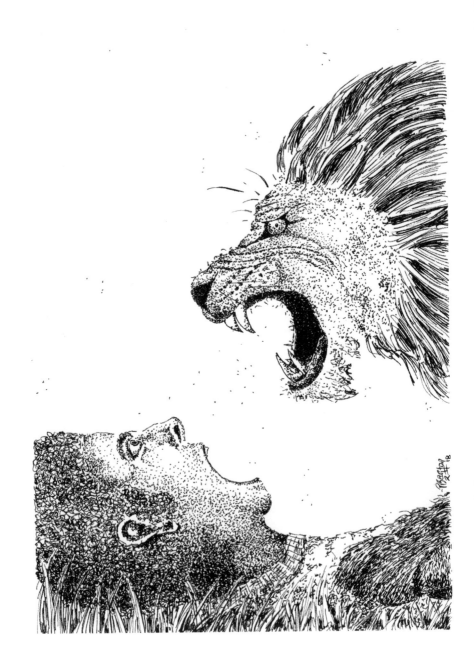

CHAPTER 18
MAN VS. BEAST

When the animals returned to Hope Haven, the uprights opened the gates. They ushered the calves inside to the safety of the courtyard. The elephant herd stood just outside the gates, unwilling to enter.

Kumani turned to them. "What's the problem?"

"We do not belong here," Beeza answered her. "We want our calves back, Kumani."

Kumani appeared to be choosing her next words carefully. "Look at them. They are terrified. They are not ready to be back on the plains with us. They need some time, Beeza. Trust me. I know."

"I think she's right," agreed Thunder. "I know what it's like to have everything you've ever known ripped out from under you. Let Imani look after them, until they feel it's safe enough to return."

Beeza looked from one to the other and let out a sigh of defeat. "Their mothers...."

Kumani looked down at the ground. "I know."

143

"Were their mothers the two elephants in the plains?" Thunder asked them. He had not even thought about it until now.

"Yes." Kumani turned to him. Her eyes were filled with tears, for she had not really allowed the grief to hit her until this moment. She had been so focused on making sure the calves were returned.

Thunder did not even think before he acted. He put his head next to hers and tried to comfort her. Kumani wrapped her trunk around his and let her tears fall to the ground. Thunder understood her grief. Losing a loved one had ripped a piece of his soul out a little at a time, until he had learned that it was a cycle each of them were destined to fulfill. They were born. They died. It was what they did in the middle of it all that made their time here on earth worth the effort of surviving in a world where the uprights seemed to have the upper hand.

"We rise. We fall." Thunder's words were soft. "We live again through the next generation."

"Yes. You're right." Kumani sniffed and pulled her trunk away to wipe her tears. "Now what do we do?"

Thunder took a moment to think. They could not take the calves yet...they were too traumatized and barely able to think. The little ones needed time to grieve. Time to come to terms with it all. "I'm going to stay. I want them to know we're here."

Kumani nodded. "Me too."

Beeza looked from Thunder to Kumani and then turned to speak with the other elephants. "We'll graze near here until our calves are ready to come home."

A few trumpets echoed around them. They were all in agreement. The herd would wait here until they could take their young home. The uprights watched them from the gates, as if trying to determine what they should do.

Thunder turned to his friends. "Are you going to stay too?"

"Of course," Razor answered. He sniffed the air and his hair rose slightly.

"What is it, Razor?" Thunder was immediately on alert.

"Probably nothing, but...." He turned his gaze to the back corner of Hope Haven, where a small pen was nestled away from the other animals inside the gates. Inside was a lioness who was licking a wound on her left paw. As if she caught his scent at the same time, her head turned up and she gazed across the distance at him.

"Is that...?" Archie started to ask him.

"A lioness," answered Thunder. He saw the goofy grin on Razor's face and chuckled. "Well...all good things come to those who wait."

"Right. No reason to leave yet." Razor cleared his throat. "Family and all that."

Thunder turned to Leopold, who was rolling his eyes at the lovesick lion next to him. "And you?"

"Me?" Leopold looked as if he were slightly shocked.

"Yes. Are you staying too?" Thunder asked him.

"You want me to stay?" Leopold could not believe what the elephant was asking him.

"Are you deaf?" Archie peered at the leopard as if he had

145

lost his mind.

"What?" Leopold was clearly having trouble putting his thoughts together. "No, of course not. I just thought you would want me to leave, seeing as how I've been trying to kill you most of your life."

"Anyone can change...." Thunder smiled at him and saw that the leopard was clearly affected by his words.

"Yes, I suppose they can." Leopold returned his smile. "I might as well stick around. I can always hunt you later, that is."

"Right." Cedric smirked at the leopard from above. His siblings were perched next to him. Not one of the egrets was buying Leopold's bold words.

As the large group of animals gathered in the plains near Hope Haven, the birds kept their eyes on the horizon. A few hours passed and all seemed to be well near them, until a small flock of sandpipers burst through the tall grasses in a clear panic. Every inch of Razor's body was now on alert.

"Uprights...."

The herd of elephants started to spook, and Kumani attempted to calm them. "You can run or you can fight. I don't know about you, but I am tired of being afraid. Today, I'm taking back my life. No upright owns it."

"I'm with you, Kumani." Thunder stood proudly next to her.

"Me too," Beeza agreed. The elephants gathered around her.

The egrets looked down at Thunder. Sydney was standing up in a fierce display of emotion. "We're not going anywhere."

146

"Let's not wait. Charge!" Kumani shouted.

The next few moments were a flurry of dust as every animal there pushed forward to where the uprights were unprepared for their arrival. Never before had a group of animals faced off with the poachers.

"What the...?" the upright Joseph called out. "Get them!"

The uprights started to raise their weapons, but the elephants did not back off. They were a massive stampede headed right toward them. The birds dive bombed them, trying to distract their aim. They were so confused they lowered the weapons and were soon overwhelmed with the charging herd.

The upright child raised his weapon as his father commanded, but he could not bring himself to shoot. His father bellowed at him. "Kill them!"

A tear fell down Pal's face. He did not want to disappoint his father, but he could not pull the trigger. Maybe it was the majestic display of the animals before them that made his conscience speak louder than his fear. "No."

"What are you doing, Pal?" His father glared at him. "Shoot!"

Pal dropped his weapon to the ground. "No. I won't do it. You can't make me."

"Can't make you? I brought you into this world boy, I can take you out of it." Joseph was so angry that he turned to face his son with his gun still in the air.

Sensing the danger, Razor leapt through the air and knocked the upright to the ground. A loud shot rang out. *Crack!* Razor felt the hot angry slice of the bullet as it lanced

147

through his thick skin, but he did not let go, nor did he attack the upright. Instead, he lay there on top of him with his eyes trained on him.

The upright looked up at him, as if knowing his judgment day had come. This lion could take his life at any moment, but instead he lay there on top of him. He didn't even try to move his head to look at his son.

The other uprights were being cornered by the angry elephants. Thunder stomped harder than he ever had, hoping to bring help from inside Hope Haven. At that moment, Imani came out of one of the larger huts. She was followed by a few uprights that Thunder did not recognize. They had small shiny badges attached to their clothing and carried weapons just like their attackers. Thunder felt a small panic rise inside him. Surely Imani would not be bringing more danger to the animals outside.

Imani pointed to the men who were being corralled successfully by the animals outside. The uprights raced over to them and raised their weapons. They shouted words that Thunder did not understand. The poachers got to their knees and put their hands behind their heads. In moments the poachers were detained as the officials that Imani had brought started to move them into large vehicles.

Imani and Daniel moved closer to Razor, who growled at them the minute they walked closer. Thunder stepped closer to his friend. "Razor…let him up."

"I can't.…" The anger in his eyes mixed with the painful haze the lion was trapped inside.

Thunder understood, but if Razor did not move, the

148

uprights would take action. They would not let an upright be killed by the lion. Thunder stepped closer to him, knowing there was only one thing he could do. He stomped on the weapon that the upright still had his hand over. The barrel broke in half and the man howled in pain. Thunder wrapped his trunk around Razor and lifted him gently from the upright beneath him. When he placed his friend on the ground, he saw the red liquid pouring from his side.

Imani noticed at the same time. "Daniel, get the tranquilizers. We have to help him."

Thunder saw Daniel race away from the group. When he returned with a weapon and pointed it at Razor, Thunder reared back on is back legs and trumpeted angrily. He would not let them hurt them. It was Kumani that brought him out of his angry haze.

"Thunder! Stop. He's not going to hurt him." Kumani stepped in front of him and touched her trunk to his head. "Do you trust me?"

Thunder blinked at her as his thoughts raced inside him. "Ugh...yes...I trust you."

"Then step away," Kumani pleaded with him.

Thunder felt his fear start to subside. He glanced at Razor, who was clearly in pain. The lion was moaning softly, and his breath came in painful gasps. Thunder did the only thing he could. Stepping away from Razor, he looked up at the sky. He put his faith in destiny, that these uprights would do what they had always promised to do, to preserve and protect all animal life.

Daniel quickly used the tranquilizer on Razor, then a few

149

of the other volunteers that worked at Hope Haven came out to gather his sleeping body. They rushed him to the large hut and Imani walked over to Thunder. She held out her hand. "Don't worry, boy. We'll patch him up better than ever."

Thunder may not have understood her words, but he knew the sentiment behind them. He wrapped his trunk around her and pulled her close to his body. Imani stroked his ear softly. As tears fell down his face, they were mirrored in her own sorrow.

"I have to go help him." Imani kissed him on his side and patted him one last time.

Thunder watched as she walked away. Kumani came closer to him and wrapped her trunk around his.

"He's going to be okay, Thunder," she whispered to him.

"He'd better be. He's my family." Thunder tried not to let his emotions take over him.

"Mine too...." Kumani put her head up against his.

Thunder closed his eyes. In this moment, he should be the happiest elephant alive. He had finally found his mate, a true love to spend the rest of his life with, but his heart was filled with fear for his friend.

"No matter what happens, I am here for you, Thunder."

He sighed aloud. "I know. I just don't want to lose anyone else."

"You won't," Kumani assured him. "Imani knows what she's doing. I have enough faith for both of us."

Thunder remained there in her embrace, comforted by her touch. Even though his fear remained, he was happier than he had been for many years. The only thing they could do was wait and see. Thunder looked up to the sky, wishing his mother could be there with him. He imagined her grace as she and the Great Tusker looked down at him from the sky. He closed his eyes and prayed for the best possible outcome.

CHAPTER 19
RECOVERY

"Well, would you look at that...." Archie watched from the fence post as Razor strolled across the small pen where he was being kept while he healed.

Kumani smiled. "You'd think he would be relaxing. It's only been a few months since his surgery."

"Well, he has to show off his new strut." Thunder smiled as he watched Razor walking with ease. For the first time in years his friend did not have the limp that had kept him from fending for himself. When the uprights had taken Razor to tend to his injury, they had discovered the other wound that had not healed well. They removed the bullets from his previous injury and gave him a little physical therapy to boost his recovery.

"Well, clearly it's working. Sasha seem quite interested," Kumani giggled when Sasha pounced on top of Razor. The two lions had been put in the same pen when Razor was healthy enough for company.

Thunder was glad to see his friend happy for a change.

153

After their epic battle with the poachers, the egrets had returned home to their families. Penelope was still inside Hope Haven tending to her little ones. Soon they would all be released back into their natural habitats.

Today the calves would be returning to the herd. Their fear had started to diminish as time helped ease their anxiety. Thunder watched them from afar. The calves were trying to play with Pasha, but the poor calf could not keep up with them. Pasha moved away from the calves and his head bowed low to the ground. The little tyke sucked his trunk into his mouth and comforted himself the only way he knew how.

It broke Thunder's heart to know that Pasha would never be in the wild with the rest of them. The herd could not protect him the way that Hope Haven could. His lack of sight would make it difficult to keep him safe. He was in far better hands here with Imani and her friends. That was the only thing that brought him comfort.

Leopold came closer to Thunder to warn him. "We have company...."

Thunder sighed heavily. "Now what?"

"Hyenas...," Leopold said with a sneer.

"Well...well...well...look who's flown the coop. Where are your loyalties, Leopold?" Delphi looked down her nose at him.

"I don't owe you anything, Delphi." Leopold held his head high.

Delphi snarled at him and her clan stepped in line behind her. "You owe me your life, you ungrateful —"

Thunder moved next to the leopard. "If you want him,

154

you have to go through me."

Delphi looked at him incredulously. "You don't scare me, Thunder."

"And me...." Kumani stepped next to him.

Delphi chuckled. "Three to our entire clan?" Her offspring was nothing compared to the line that had joined her. Delphi was confident that they would be able to win the fight. That was until Kumani's entire herd joined the ranks.

"You hurt one of us...you fight all of us." Thunder stomped threateningly on the ground and a chorus of loud angry trumpets echoed around them.

Delphi sniffed at him. "Well, you don't have to get your tusks twisted."

"Leave now, Delphi, and know that if you ever come back, we will end this once and for all." Thunder was not going to back down. He had finally had enough of these vile creatures. Thunder stomped so hard that the hyenas bounced off the ground. A few of them yelped in fear before they fled from the scene.

Leopold chuckled loudly. "I've never seen them run so fast before."

Thunder laughed with him. "That's true. They could give you a run for your money."

Leopold sobered up as he turned to face him. "Thank you...."

"I meant what I said. We protect our own. That includes you."

Leopold blinked his eyes as if he had dust caught inside them. He swiped at his eyes and sniffed. "Allergies...dust in my eyes and all that."

"Right." Thunder smiled and looked over at his mate. Kumani returned it with her own. He could not help but think about how much his life had changed. Thunder was happier than he ever thought he deserved to be. His life was so much more fulfilling than he had ever dreamed it would be.

***

Delphi was in a foul mood when she entered their cave. They had been away from it for the past few weeks while they had followed after the upright poachers. Their free meal ticket had been a bust. The clans that had followed her no longer had faith in her direction. As of today, she was no longer ruler of the clans.

"Stupid ingrates…," she growled.

Her children followed her into the cave, no one bothering to say a word, for they knew the wrath of Delphi quite well. As they moved further into the darkness, a whisper of movement echoed around them.

"What was that?" Jack asked fearfully.

"Nothing, you idiot," Delphi snapped at him.

Two eyes opened in the darkness. The orbs glowed ever so slightly. "Someone needs to learn some manners."

"What in the…?" Delphi barely got her words out as something sharp grazed her leg. "Ah! Run!"

The hyenas wasted no time fleeing the cave. As they raced through the tunnels, more glowing eyes appeared. "I think this cave's occupied!" Tara called out.

The hyenas were chased from the cave by a bask of orange crocodiles. Their leader, Princess Gabriella, was at the head of the attack. "And don't come back!" she called after the yelping creatures who were grabbing at various appendages as they raced away.

CHAPTER 20
TWO YEARS LATER

The sun tried to break through the dark clouds above as the storm made itself known to the world below. The smell of rain teased the air. Today was a special day. All the animals of the rainforest, friends and family alike, had gathered to witness the miracle that was about to happen. Thunder and Kumani were expecting their first child.

Each animal had brought a gift to lay at their feet. Riley had left the beach behind just to see this special day. He lay shells at Thunder's feet to help welcome the baby into this world. The egrets had brought shiny rocks they had traded Frederick for, and had made a large strand on the ground. They watched from their perches in the tree.

Neville and Harold place a bunch of bananas at his feet. "Best of luck, my boy."

Salem had also come back to greet him. He lay a wreath of flowers down before them. "My mother would have wanted me here."

Thunder smiled warmly at him. "Thank you, Salem."

The genets were no longer kits and soon would have families of their own. They had gathered fruits and vegetables to give Kumani sustenance during her labor.

"Is he here yet?" Khari called out anxiously. He was like a proud uncle, waiting to see the baby for the first time.

"Relax. These things take time," Ayo answered. She rubbed her enlarged belly gently as the life within her moved as if to illustrate her point. Ayo had already found her own mate. Khari had yet to settle down.

Dash smiled at his offspring. "Patience. Soon...."

When Khari stopped racing around, he was tackled by a small ball of fluff. "Naya!"

The lion cub chewed on his ear playfully before Razor pulled her off. "Come here, little one." Razor carried his cub back over to Sasha, who was grooming his son, Aesop. "This one got away."

"Come here, you." Sasha pulled her close when Razor dropped her down. Her eyes met his and they were filled with the same adoration echoed in his own.

Archie's eyes were filled with tears as he gave them a loopy smile. He lay a few berry-covered branches at his friends' feet. "Many blessings on this day."

Thunder nodded to the lizard and turned back to Kumani. "It's almost time, my love."

A loud boom shattered the silence and rain fell down on their heads. The sun flickered on and off between the clouds as they floated overhead. A steady stream fell from the sky, as if cleansing the birth of the tiny calf below. The herd moved around Kumani as a tiny calf emerged from her belly and dropped slowly to the ground.

Tears filled her eyes as she waited for the calf to take its first breath. When a tiny trumpet called out below her, she finally breathed a sigh of relief. "Come up, you."

Both parents tried to help their son stand. He took a tiny step forward, and when thunder echoed around them again, the calf stomped his foot in time. A small rumble shook the ground, and Thunder beamed in pride.

"Like father, like son." Kumani looked at the herd around her. "Meet Thunder, Junior."

The herd rumbled softly together, their feet stamping their pride as they welcomed new life to the world around them. They raised their trunks to the sky and sang their joy to the skies above. The tiny calf tried to shake his feet like the elders and fell over his own feet. He shook his head and snorted through his trunk. Thunder Junior did not let that keep him down though. He stood up with his awkward legs and tried to rumble like the adults again. His tiny trembles were enough to make any parent proud.

Thunder looked up in the sky. The dark clouds had parted and lighter ones passed them by. There in the puffy white heavens above, Thunder saw one face looking down at him. Serenity beamed down at her son and grandchild, the love reflected through her face as beautiful streams of light filtered through the air and surrounded the world below. Thunder felt the gentle glow of her love and knew that his greatest destiny was this moment in time, when he had brought new life to their world. A new cycle would begin, as one rises and falls. Everything has a beginning and end. From here, only the Great Tusker in the sky knew where his son's path would lead.

The End

About the Author

Erik Daniel Shein was born Erik Daniel Stoops, November 18th 1966. He is an American writer, and visionary, film producer, screenwriter, voice actor, animator, entrepreneur, entertainer, and philanthropist, pet enthusiast and animal health advocate. He is the author and co-author of over 30 nonfiction and fiction books whose writings include six scientific articles in the field of herpetology. His children's book, "The Forgotten Ornament" is a Christmas classic, and was endorsed by Hollywood legends Mickey and Jan Rooney.

Author credits: Animated Film "The Legend of Secret Pass"
https://www.youtube.com/watch?v=SPUJy2DYRZw
http://www.imdb.com/title/tt0765465/combined
http://www.malcolminthemiddle.co.uk/2007/06/20/
frankie-muniz-the-legend-of-secret-pass-movie/

About the Author

Born in Southern Illinois, Melissa Davis fell in love with reading from an early age, so much so that she started writing when she was in the second grade. From poetry, to short stories, she has a love for it all. When she was in high school she attended Illinois Summer School for the Arts at Illinois State University, which lead her to attend the university. After graduating with a Bachelors in Education, Melissa taught for several years until her children were born, allowing her to fulfill two dreams at once: motherhood and penning her first books.

CPSIA information can be obtained
at www.ICGtesting.com
Printed in the USA
LVHW040925201218
600896LV00002B/209/P

9 781629 896304